Theodore F. Lee brings to the writing world a wonderful vision, influenced by countless occupations. His writing material has been chiselled from a colourful palette of life experiences, that took this author from the hard labor of fishing rooms to the hallowed halls of university classrooms. Merging from those many experiences, he reconstructs a literary picture that excites the imagination with the turn of each page and the conclusion from every chapter. Even though Theodore has achieved multiple university degrees that include a master's in education, he believes that the true path for a fulfilled life comes from the space between pages of life.

To my wife Alana, who is not only my best friend but is also my guiding hand when my words become too ambitious. To my two daughters Jessica and Meaghan, who's support I appreciate more than they would ever know. And finally, to my remaining family, who I can always lean upon, when the winds of Conception Bay become too strong to handle.

Theodore F. Lee

THE SECRET SACRAMENT

AUSTIN MACAULEY PUBLISHERS™
LONDON • CAMBRIDGE • NEW YORK • SHARJAH

Ordering Information
Quantity sales: Special discounts are available on quantity purchases by corporations, associations, and others. For details, contact the publisher at the address below.

Publisher's Cataloging-in-Publication data
Lee, Theodore F.
The Secret Sacrament

ISBN 9781685623227 (Paperback)
ISBN 9781685623234 (ePub e-book)

Library of Congress Control Number: 2023909159

www.austinmacauley.com/us

First Published 2023
Austin Macauley Publishers LLC
40 Wall Street 33rd Floor, Suite 3302
New York, NY 10005
USA

mail-usa@austinmacauley.com
+1 (646) 5125767

Table of Contents

Chapter 1

The Diminished Flame

Pat Morey walked slowly up the steps and stopped on the landing in front of the door. He peeped through the screen and shouted, "FATHER MALONE...THE FIRE IS READY..." The priest laid his hands on the freshly-pressed vestments and placed them gently into the box. He looked up at the wooden cross that hung on the bare wall and shouted back, "THANK YOU PAT, I'll be there in a few minutes..." Pat Morey turned around quickly and rushed off to stoke the flaming fire that raged in the rusty barrel.

Father Malone meticulously folded each vestment and laid them into a shallow box with punctilious precision. The Chasuble, yoke of unselfish love, was gently placed to the bottom of the box with great reverence. Next came the Alb and the Amice that were also softly laid down to rest upon the virtue garment of charity. Finally, Father Malone took the symbol of his official liturgical role from the bed and placed the white, blood-soaked stole inside the wooden box. With his precious vestments safely packed, the priest put the lid on the box and slowly carried it downstairs, where his brother Damian waited at the bottom rail.

"You haven't got much time to waste Peter, if you want to catch that plane tonight…" Father Peter Malone placed the wooden box upon the side table with his bloodied hands, and asked, "Do we have time for a cup of tea?" Damian stared at his brother's broken eyes and said, "Why don't you wash your hands and then we'll have a chat."

While Peter washed away the blood from his pale palms, he began to mumble, "That being cleansed from all stain, I might serve you with purity of mind and soul." From the far corner of the room, Damian heard Father Malone's humble prayer and responded with clenched teeth, "Well Peter…They'll never get the stain off their souls, no matter how hard those bastards wash their hands…" Father Malone looked at his brother with a blank stare and waved him into the kitchen without responding. Placing the kettle upon the stove he finally spoke, "Not all priests play into the hands of the devil, my dear brother." Realizing, he may have gone too far, Damian responded, "Maybe not all Peter…But you only need a few bad apples, to spoil the whole pie…"

Father Peter slowly nodded his head, and sadly said, "But in the past, many good souls placed their lives on the line, to spread the word…In a world bad to the core—"

Without hesitation, Damian quickly retorted, "And now…They're rolling in their cold coffins knowing what these rotten bastards have done to their fragile flock."

Too weakened by the sad string of events that recently occurred, Father Peter poured out the tea and placed it in front of his brother. With the sugar bowl in hand and a fragile smile on his face, he asked, "Will you forgive me, for my sins of the past?"

Damian smirked, shook his head, and replied, "If you're talking about my hasty departure from our home, well…you, my dear brother, are not to blame." He took a sip of tea and continued, "You were only a kid, blinded by what you believed in…You couldn't see what happened to me."

Father Peter Malone stirred his tea deeply and said, "Yes, I suppose you're right…"

Damian carefully measured his brother's sullen movements, and with great reverence he asked, "What happened to you Brother? Why did you become a priest?"

Father Peter Malone removed his white collar, placed in on the table, "I believed that I was called."

Damian squirmed on the chrome kitchen chair and asked, "Called by who?"

There was a moment of silence with only the sound of the clock pushing the hands of time, and then Father Peter slowly looked up from his cup, "Well…I didn't know at the time, that many were called but few were chosen."

Damian considered the pain upon his brother's face and said, "You know what I think about your holy brothers…It goes without saying, especially considering today's funeral service…But if there was one good priest, that could lay my soul at rest…it would be you…" Before Father Peter could say a word, Damian added, "As for the rest of those perverts, well they can all rot in hell."

"Thank you for your vote of confidence, but there are many more good priests than they are bad."

"Don't you think they should stand up for the weak and the ones who can't speak for themselves?"

"It's a complicated web of circumstances that goes deeper than what I know."

"Well Peter, it's time they shed some light on that dark web of suspicion."

"I know you don't understand Damian, but I tried…And I failed…And it's my fault…"

"Don't even go there…It's only the fault of those perverts and the ones that supported them…You tried to open the eyes of those blind bastards."

Without an ounce of anger in his voice, Father Peter said, "We must forgive their sins."

Damian opened his eyes to full capacity, and said sharply, "We? Don't ask me to forgive those guilty pricks…I'd hang them, like they hung that poor innocent kid."

It was too much for Father Peter Malone to hear and it was too late for Damian to shut a crude mouth that spewed the gospel truth. Realizing complete honesty was the only way to help his brother, Damian laid his hands on the table, and asked, "What really happened to that young boy, Peter?"

Father Peter stood up, removed his black jacket and placed it with his white collar on top of the wooden box. For one moment, he stood and stared at a bright green sweater that hung on a hook in the dark hall. Slowly, he pulled it over his crisp white shirt and returned to the table and asked, "Would you like more tea?"

Damian pushed the cup to the side, shook his head and said, "I would prefer the truth…"

Peter sat down at the table, unbuttoned his stiff shirt, and asked with a deep sigh, "What is truth Damian?"

"Truth…Is that sweater you're wearing on your back that says Ireland on the front."

"Maybe so…But the truth can't bring back an innocent soul…"

"True…But it can prevent the loss of more innocent souls."

Peter took off his shiny black shoes and flicked them towards the side table. He opened the box, that Damian had placed on the table, and removed a pair of white sneakers. Placing them on his feet, he looked up at his brother and said, "The river runs deep Damian…"

Damian placed his head in his hands for a second and then looked over at Peter. With frustration in his voice, he said, "Enough with the mumbo jumbo…Don't feed their ambiguous bullshit, Peter!"

Peter Malone looked at the most true-blue person he had ever known, and replied, "When I called you two days ago and explained what happened, you did not hesitate…You boarded a plane and came to my side." Peter looked at the small pine box sitting at the bottom of stairs and said, "You have been the rock that I must build my life upon…A solid rock of truth based on the belief in myself…"

While Damian watched his brother slip on his fresh new sneakers, he inquired, "Those are strong words Peter…But why did you change direction?" Without waiting for a reply, he asked, "Was it the road to Dublin?"

Before he could answer, there was a soft knock on the door, followed by a meek voice asking for Father Peter Malone.

Father Stephen walked in and stepped back in a startled stare. The casual appearance of his former seminary student had caught him off guard. With a sincere bow of the head, he said, "I see this ordeal has affected you deeply, Father Peter." Blessing himself, he hauled out his beads and began to recite the rosary, until Damian interrupted, "There's no need of any long-winded confessions now…There'll be plenty of time to tell your story to the courts…Right now, this man has a plane to catch."

"Plane?" Father Stephen asked.

Father Peter began to explain, "I was going to tell you later, about my plans…"

Without allowing Peter to continue, Damian butted in, "You don't owe this jack ass any explanation…"

Without allowing Damian to continue, Peter butted in strongly, "This jack ass is my friend, and is the salt of the earth."

Grasping the strained look upon his brother's face, Damian realized he had tread on holy ground. He quickly retreated back down onto his seat, without further defense for his holy brother.

In the company of a lay person, Father Stephen deemed it best to steer the conversation away from personal debate and towards the business at hand. Ignoring any further visual distractions, Father Stephen said, "The funeral service went very smooth, considering the sad circumstances…" Damian fired off a quick stare at his brother and found a shielding shake of a head that signaled a silent response. Father Stephen pickup up on the frosty reception and carefully continued, "Before I leave…I have just one question…"

"In your homily, you spoke of finding one's individual truth…Before it was too late…" Father Stephen placed the rosary beads back into the chamber of his pocket, and asked, "Father Peter, what did you mean?"

Peter Malone picked up his cup, finding it empty, he laid it back down on the table, and said, "Not everyone finds truth, until it is too late. We had the responsibility of innocent souls in our hands, and we failed to grasp the truth. This tragedy could have been prevented if only we had accepted the truth of what, we have become."

Listening intently, Father Stephen softy said, "You cast a wide net Brother. Surely, we are not all to blame, for the actions of a few."

Father Peter heard his fellow priest plainly, and responded, "But we share the blame with our silence…"

Father Stephen sat down by the side of Father Peter, and asked, "Then, where do we go from here?"

Father Peter nodded his head and replied, "Go out and spread the word."

Baffled by the simplicity of the message, Father Stephen lowered his eyebrows and asked, "The word of God?" He leaned closer and added, "To the flock?"

With a slow shake of his head, Father Peter replied, "A change of guard is needed…for the Shepherds…"

Still puzzled by the answer, Father Stephen asked, "What Shepherds?"

Damian had been silent long enough. He had given them time to talk and now it was his turn to clarify the facts. "Let me translate for my brother, Brother…" Peter held his hand in front of him, but Damian couldn't help spewing out, "The Shepherds are the high-hat ass-holes, who sit on their thrones and make the decisions cloaked in secrecy and deceit." With Peter's hand lowered, Damian continued,

"The word is clear, my holy brother. The people will no longer tolerate the opulence of wealth gained at the expense of broken backs and will not stand by, while sexual gratification is perpetrated on innocent children…" Damian sat back slowly in his chair and asked, "Is that truth, clear enough for you, holy brother?"

With distorted strain upon Father Peter's face, Damian and Father Stephen could see the tragic event unfold before their very eyes at the kitchen table. The fresh sacrificed wounds from the blood of an innocent boy had pierced the soul of a priest who searched for meaning of truth and found nothing but pure lies.

Father Peter placed his head in his hands, mistakenly giving Father Stephen a signal to bless himself, and say, "We must pray for the soul of the young boy who committed suicide."

Without warning Peter struck the hard kitchen table with his soft fist, sending cups and spoons to the four corners of the room. The startled men stood back watched the frustrated priest place his hands out straight, and exclaim, "He didn't commit a crime or a sin! He died by suicide." Peter spread his hands out to the sides, and continued in a softer voice, "He sacrificed his life, so others could see the truth…"

Father Stephen finished blessing himself, and said, "And we will help spread the word of truth to our Bishop."

Damian rolled his eyes at Peter, then Father Peter said, "You will only find pushback and unwillingness from your Bishop."

Father Stephen stood in the doorway and exclaimed, "But he is your Bishop, Father Peter!"

Stoked up like a raging fire, Damian shouted, "He's a self-righteous prick!" It was too late for Peter to pour cold water on Damian's flaming rage. He continued to smolder, "That shriveled up shyster, knew all about those priestly perverts and what they did to those innocent boys."

Father Stephen stepped in, and asked Peter, "Did you know this?"

"Yes, I tried to address it at the seminary retreat, but they wouldn't listen."

"Maybe you weren't clear enough…"

"I stood up and told them the young boy was raped…"

Damian stood between the two priests and sarcastically weighed in with his support, "Sounds pretty clear to me, Father Stephen."

Trying to make sense of what he had heard, Father Stephen softly said, "He's only a man, and men make many mistakes…"

Damian shook his head and said, "That's not a mistake Brother…That was turning a blind eye to the plain truth, which makes him a monster, not a man."

Father Peter went in front of Father Stephen and grabbed his shoulders and said, "Stephen, place your faith in no man."

Father Stephen asked, "Then who…If not Bishop Murphy?"

With a puzzled look, Peter said, "You have it mixed up…Bishop Stone is the Bishop…not Monsignor Murphy…"

"No, I'm sure Father King told me it was Bishop Murphy."

Suddenly, there was a knock on the door and the mistaken identity of the Bishop was put aside. Pat Morey walked into the kitchen, and said, "Father Malone your fire is ready."

Damian reached over with his outstretched hand and said, "Sorry for your loss, sir."

Pat shook his hand, and replied, "He was my only son..." Father Stephen placed his hand out with a sincere, "He's in heaven now..." Pat ignored his hand, and said, "The wound is fresh Father, and my soul is weak."

Father Peter placed his arm around his good friend, and said, "You are a strong man Pat Morey, and your faith is stronger than any man I know."

Pat Morey cleared his throat looked at Father Peter, and asked, "What did you want with the fire, Father?"

Peter looked towards Damian and asked, "Could you hold the door for me?" Picking up the box of vestments and his outer garments Father Peter Malone answered Pat Morey, by saying, "I'm going to cleanse my soul, Pat..." Without further discussion, Peter went through the opened door holding everything he had previously believed in.

Outside, the blazing fire licked the sides of the rusty iron barrel as the men approached. For a moment, they stopped in front of the fire and then without warning, Father Peter Malone threw his outer garments upon the raging flame. Two wide-eyed men stood in silent shock, while the other man swatched his brother remove the weight of the world from his soul.

Peter opened the wooden box, placed the bloodied stole to the side and was about to throw the items into the burning barrel, when Father Stephan placed his hands upon the sacred garments. Picking up the Amice, Father Stephen said, "This is the garment to repel assaults of the devil." Peter looked at his former college, and replied, "It is only cloth…and has been worn by the guilty priests, to pull in the innocent victims and destroy their lives." Sliding the garment from Father Stephen's loosened hands, he threw it on the flickering fire. The three men watched Peter Malone clutch the blood-soaked stole with an absent look upon his face. In the reflection of the rusty fire, Peter had become detached with the present and transfixed on a time gone by. Father Peter Malone could no longer feel the heat from the barrel or listen to the echoes of tragedy. Peter could only hear his father's voice, calling from a past, where sacred secrets where just beginning.

Chapter 2

Sparks of Spiritualty

"DAMIAN! STOP FANNING THAT FIRE!" Gus Malone quickly picked up his younger son and carried him away from the flying sparks. He laid him down gently on the nearby log, turned to his older son and said, "What's wrong with you boy?"

"I was just trying to stoke the fire, that's all."

"Well, if those sparks had scorched your brother, you'd be wearing the print of your mother's hand when we got home."

Gus had dropped his guard for one minute to get a shallow bucket of water from the fishing pond and almost found himself in trouble with his deeply religious wife. With the loss of their five sons, due to a tragic boating accident, young Peter represented the jewel in the Holy Grail and her shining hope of salvation. Born the seventh son of a seventh son, Mary Malone believed that little boy had the potential of pulling them out of purgatory and into the arms of the angels. One misplaced spark landing on her chosen child, could have landed the original seventh son outside their sacred circle and into a hole of damnation.

Damian sat close to the fire and watched from a distance, at the contented look upon his father's face. Out in the woods, away from the constant scourging of scrutiny and criticism, they were almost on common ground. In a house pushing for sanctimonious perfection, the freedom of the woods provided a peace of mind from the confines of their strict religious world. Even though the space between each brother was different, Damian was willing to accept his place by the fire, if only he could stay under the arms of the protective forest.

With the youngest child safely by his side, Gus said, "Your mother will be worried about Peter. It's time we get home." Damian ignored the thought of returning home and defiantly responded by grabbing another green branch to fan the fire. Before the smoldering fire could be redeemed, Gus Malone threw a bucket of cold water over the remaining embers and Damian's hope of staying one second longer. As the ascending white smoke billowed up through the reluctant trees, Gus Malone lumbered along with Peter on his back and Damian in the rear. Trudging slowly behind, he said.

"Why can't we stay, Pop?"

"Everything comes to an end boy."

"Not if you don't want it, Pop."

"What I want, don't matter boy…"

"Matters to me…"

Mr. Malone stopped for a second and said, "Thanks son, but the only opinion matters is your mother's. Now, let's get going, before she starts lighting candles for us."

Mary Malone heard the door opening and without hesitation, she shouted, "What the blue blazes kept you so long?" She quickly latched on to young Peter and removed him from his father's shoulders. Placing him on the chair, she said, "It's time we said the Rosary." Without thinking, Damian unwittingly blurted out, "But, we just got home…" Too late. He had spoken out within the range of his mother's arm, and quickly found the back of her hand across his open mouth. Gus Malone shook his head, dropped to his knees and began, "Our Father who art in heaven…"

Right in the middle of Gus Malone's reluctant introduction of the rosary, Mary Malone exclaimed, "WAIT!" She blessed herself, and continued, "We will offer this rosary up to the poor men aboard the Apollo 13 mission." Gus quickly stood up, went to the television and turned on a black and white image of Walter Cronkite, saying, "Houston, we have a problem." Young Damian couldn't help himself, when he mumbled, "And they're not the only ones…" Mary Malone quickly asked her son, "What did you say?"

Damian pretended to close his eyes and mumbled louder, "Holy Mary full of grace…" She returned her attention to her husband and demanded, "Turn that off and let's continue with the Rosary."

He turned off the small television and asked, "What happened?"

"They had an incident aboard the spacecraft."

"Are they dead?"

"No, but they soon will be in the arms of the Lord."

"The poor men…"

"Well, I don't know if the Holy See agrees with men going into space."

Gus softly suggested, "I'm not sure, if that's how the church sees it now." With a sharp look from Mary for clarification, Gus continued gently, "I read in this morning's paper, the Bishop of Orlando reported to the Pope, that the moon lands within their diocese." Young Damian couldn't control his mumbling when he whispered to his father, "More money for the collection plate." Gus knew Mary couldn't hear him, but he shook his head and softly pinched Damian's arm out of site from his kneeing wife. Mary Malone took a quick look into little Peter's crystal blue eyes, kissed him on the cheek, and said, "Well, if the Pope is on board, then we are with him." With her finger pointing directly at the floor, Gus Malone crumbled to his knees, and began again, "Our Father who art in heaven..."

The next day, after Sunday mass, Father Jim Piercy greeted Gus Malone with a soft handshake and a request he couldn't refuse. With Mary Malone shoulder to shoulder with her husband, Father Piercy suggested, "There will be visiting priests from the archdiocese coming this week and I would like to bring them over to your house for tea." Watching the glow on his wife's face, Gus Malone tightened his handshake a little too much, and replied, "Of course Father, we'd love to have them over." Gus Malone released the priest's imprinted hand, while Father Piercy turned his cheek to greet the fleeing flock.

Just as the Malone family had shuffled out the door Father Piercy latched on to his close friend, hauled him back in, and said quietly, "Sorry for putting you on the spot Gus, but I really needed your help with this." Gus leaned in with a smile, and in a low voice he replied, "Don't worry Jim, I'll forgive you for your sins."

Father Jim grinned, and suggested, "You better keep the silver tea set out of site, or they'll pick your pockets clean Gus…" Pretending to be upset with an exaggerated scowl, Gus sighed sarcastically, and whispered, "You're the devil's helper Jim."

On the following Friday, the Malones were left in limbo, waiting for the arrival of the three proper priests. The floors had been waxed and the walls had been washed with great attention to detail, until it all gleamed with Mary Malone's pride. Even the children were scrubbed until they were rubbed red raw and ready for the holy siege. There was nothing else to do, except sit in one spot, without disturbing anything from its pristine place.

To the delight of Mary Malone, Father Piercy finally arrived in the afternoon with his holy colleagues. The three priests were paraded through the house with the regular pomp and ceremony that came with such high-profile guests. Glancing from corner to corner, the two high priests scanned every nook and cranny, as they slowly walked through the Malone's humble house seeking items of interest. "I love the hardwood floor Mrs. Malone, must have been expensive," said the taller priest with the square biretta.

"Yes…The stained glass in the front door is quite exquisite," said the other shorter priest, as he coughed.

In short, they were crammed into the little living room where the three priests sat, surrounded by the Malone family. While Mary Malone quickly scurried off to prepare tea for her guests, Gus Malone began to speak, "I heard this morning, that Apollo astronauts have made it around the moon and are heading back home." The taller priest responded with a simple, "Well, it's all in God's hands now."

From the back of the room, fifteen-year-old Damian spoke, "It's in mission controls hands too Father…"

Before any further debate could be explored, Mary Malone came in with the tea and biscuits and said, "I apologize for the china, but for some reason, my silver set is missing." The shorter priest coughed, and said, "Sliver you say…My, that's a pity." Father Jim Piercy and Gus Malone traded a quick glance followed by a trace of a contained smile. With a quick wink from Father Piercy, Gus Malone excused himself and left the room thinking he had avoided a cash grab with the aid of his old friend. Off they went towards the nearby shed to have a smoke and friendly chat, leaving Mrs. Malone at the mercy of the two high priests.

Noticing that the absence of Mr. Malone presented a window of opportunity, the taller priest said, "On the way in, I noticed the framed coin collection on your wall." He leaned out towards the door to ensure they were gone, and followed with a quick question, "By any chance, does Mr. Malone have more of those beautiful coins?"

The shorter priest acknowledged the maneuver and swiftly took the discreet hint from his holy colleague. He coughed in the face of young Peter Malone and said, "My, my, aren't you a site for sore eyes."

Mrs. Malone's eyes lit up with delight by the adoration of her beloved son, and responded, "Yes, Father, I do believe he has more of those coins put away for savings."

Realizing he had hit a soft spot, the shorter priest asked the taller priest, "Doesn't he have a holy glow, Father?" Without missing a beat, the taller priest replied with confidence, "Indeed he does..." Knowing their golden opportunity may dissipate with the return of Mr. Malone, the taller priest pounced, by politely asking, "May we see those lovely coins Mrs. Malone?"

In her state of ecstasy, from the attention given to her special child, Mary Malone said, "Damian, go and get your father's coins for the good priests." From the back of the room, Damian didn't like the way the priests were digging, and quickly responded. "Maybe I should get Pop to find them."

The shorter priest rubbed young Peter's head and said, "We really would love to see those coins, Mrs. Malone."

"Go to our room and get them now!"

"But Mom, I don't know where they are?"

Before Mary Malone could take action towards her hesitant child, young Peter piped up and softly said, "I know where they are Mom, I'll get them."

The shorter priest looked at young Peter, coughed and said, "You're going to make a good priest someday."

Young Peter scurried off to get the coins and Damian rushed off to find his unsuspecting father. Within seconds, Peter returned with a large heavy bag of silver coins and placed them on the coffee table in front of the drooling priests. Gus Malone's lifetime of saving silver was shining brightly for all to see. The taunting view from the opened bag, encouraged the shorter priest to exclaim. "What a glow!" The taller priest quickly added, "Yes, indeed...The glow is breathtaking." Thinking the priests were still focused on her golden child, proud Mary Malone said, "Thank you Father." With a tight grip on the bag of coins, the short priest coughed and said, "No Mrs. Malone, thank you for your donation. Your generosity will not be forgotten at the altar."

"But…I didn't mean to give—"

"Thanks to the almighty?" The taller priest snapped.

"But…I don't think Mr. Malone would—"

"Want to see the church supported?" The shorter priest spurted.

"Yes, I do…but…"

"Of course you do Mrs. Malone…" Both priests politely replied.

With a death grip on the silver, the shorter priest coughed and said, "You'll be rewarded in heaven, Mrs. Malone."

Making sure their getaway would be clean, the two priests slipped on their square hats and slithered through the hall with Gus Malone's silver tucked close to their chests. As they went through the doorway, the shorter priest strongly suggested, "Don't forget to light a candle before mass, they're only five dollars…" There was no time to wait for formal farewells or Father Piercy. The dark-clothed men quickly boarded the black car and were gone, leaving Gus Malone with an empty bag and Mary Malone full of hope.

Gus, Damian and Father Piercy finally returned to find the two high-hated priests missing. Watching the dim taillights and descending dust from the shiny black car, Gus Malone asked the inevitable, "Did you give them our silver coins, Mary?"

"Well…I think I did…"

"What were you thinking Mary?"

Mary Malone looked over at young Peter, who gave out a slight cough, and said, "It was for the archdiocese and for hope…" Gus sat down on the kitchen chair and said sadly, "Hope for what?" With a far-away look in her eyes, she replied, "That, we may see a priest in our family."

Father Piercy's devastated face said more than any lengthy apology. Gus clearly understood that his old friend didn't realize the sharpness of their teeth, or the depth they would sink to increase the coffers of the church. Gus knew his good friend was a true man of faith and would give his life and limb for his religion and fellow man. Looking down at Father Jim's old worn-out shoes, Gus Malone said, "It wasn't your fault Jim. You didn't know they were sharks."

"No, not sharks…But I did know they could bite…and I left them alone with lambs."

Gus Malone placed out his big hand to shake, and said, "It's only money Jim…" And with a tight handshake, they agreed to meet as usual after Sunday mass.

Sunday came, but the Malone's were not in their regular seats at the church service. Father Piercy became so concerned with the missing Malone family that he decided to make a wellness call. Driving to the Malone's home, Father Piercy considered their absence in church could be related to the stolen coins. However, when he entered the kitchen, Mary Malone's fallen face told him, he was just in time.

"We were just going to call you Father Jim…It's Peter…He's not well…"

"But I saw him on Friday, and he was fine…"

"He started with a faint cough and now it seems to be in his lungs."

Mary couldn't contain herself anymore, as she broke down saying, "God can't take my Peter, Father Jim. He just can't…"

Father Piercy took Mary's hand and replied, "He works in mysterious ways my child…And maybe there's a way I can help." With quick instructions for Damian to fetch his bag from the car, Father Piercy said, "Bring me to the boy."

Gus greeted his friend with a deep nod and a shallow smile, as he held on to young Peter's small hand. Looking down at his young son, he said, "He's getting sicker by the second, Jim."

Father Piercy opened his bag, hauled out the holy water, and replied, "Not if I have anything to do with it, Gus…" Placing his hands over young Peter, they recited the Rosary and then finally Father Jim gently blessed the boy with holy water. While Father Piercy laid his hands upon his forehead, young Peter opened his eyes, and softly said, "I'm thirsty…"

His mother quickly retreated to get some water, while the men walked out into the kitchen for tea.

Mary poured out the tea, laid Father Jim's favorite tea biscuits in front of him, and said, "Father Jim, that boy is very special."

"All children are special Mary."

"But Father Jim, I think he's destined for the priesthood."

"If he is destined to be a priest, only He will know and nobody else."

Understanding the Mary's quest to put Peter on the path to holiness, Father Jim reached out and said, "Look…When the boy turns fourteen, I'll make him an altar boy. Maybe he can find his own path at that time…"

Mary Malone poured Father Jim's tea and with a wide grin, as she said, "Thank you, Father."

Father Jim sipped his tea, sat back on his chair and sarcastically asked, "What about Damian…Is he special too?"

Gus Malone snickered, and replied, "Oh he's special alright." Mary Malone got up from the table, leaving Gus to dissect the differences between the boys. "Well, he's been an altar boy with me for a few years now…And I think that boy is just as special as those visiting priests who almost got away with your silver coins."

"Almost?"

"Yes…Almost."

Gus laughed and said, "Well, my empty drawer tells me, that they did get away with my coins."

Father Jim reached over, grabbed a match from the table and lit up his pipe. Sending the smell of tobacco throughout the room, he explained, "I spoke to Monsignor Murphy about the visiting priests and their misappropriation of your funds." With a large puff of smoke he continued, "His holiness assured me it was a misunderstanding and sent back the coins to my parish to be deemed with, at my discretion." Father Jim tapped his pipe on the table and said, "Your coins are ready for you down at the church."

"I'll send down Damian later, to pick them up."

Father Jim smirked and asked, "Do you have them counted?"

Gus laughed and replied, "Between your preying priests and our Damian, I'm sure the load will be lighter."

As Gus and Mary walked out through the door with Father Piercy, Mary said, "Father Jim, we have a lot to be thankful for, with Peter feeling better…" Gus added, "And our coins coming back…" Father Jim nodded in agreement, stopped for second, and said, "I also heard on the radio that the Apollo spacecraft splashed down safely in the Pacific today." With a tip of his hat, Father Jim finally said, "Looks like God worked his mysterious ways for the good of science too."

Chapter 3

Sacristy of Sarcasm

The following year, during Easter festivities, the Malone family was celebrating Peter's fourteenth birthday. Another year had come and gone with the same rigorous routine of devout devotion within the Malone household. But on this day, the regular routine was detained for the opening of a very special gift that contained a very significant meaning for Mary Malone. With great pride, Peter's mother passed over the gift and said, "It's time we take the first step towards your dream."

Young Peter placed the box upon his knees and quickly tore off the purple wrapping. Opening the cover, his eyes danced in delight with the sight of a red cassock and white surplice. However, not everyone in the household was jumping for joy when the box was opened. His brother Damian's face dropped with disappointment, when Peter's cassock and surplice were flashed in front of his face. He knew, with his brother's new cassock, his time as an alternative altar boy would be coming to an end. Damian understood very well, that the secret tasting of wine and the tomfoolery antics of his fellow altar boys, would be unveiled by the introduction of such a vigilant guardian.

Peter quickly pulled the cassock over his head, leaving Mrs. Malone to look at Damian, and ask, "Doesn't that look smart on Peter?"

Damian shrugged his shoulders and answered, "A bike would look better…" Mrs. Malone studied his face for any sign of smart-aleck nonsense, but on that joyous occasion, she decided to place a temporary moratorium on further response. She shrugged her shoulders in frustration, and said, "Go get ready for Mass."

It was holy Sunday, and the day they had waited for all year. The time had arrived, that Peter would finally step onto Father Piercy's altar, ready for divine dedication in the service of God. Gus Malone was in the shed when Damian walked in with his head down. He sat by the side of his father and shrugged his shoulders in wonderment. Looking at his wilted face, Mr. Malone asked, "What's wrong boy, can't take the heat in the kitchen?" Damian looked at the floor, and replied, "I don't like what they're serving up, Pop."

"Well Son, I find it a bit hard to swallow myself."

"Why don't Mom let Peter figure it out for himself?"

"She's just trying to help him achieve his dream, I guess…"

"I think it's more Mom's dream, than Peter's."

Gus Malone placed his hand on his older son and said, "You better keep that talk to yourself, boy, or your mother will make minced meat from your thick hide."

Out in the front yard, Mary Malone paced back and forth, until she hollered, "GUS! GUS!" Gus quickly roared back, "I'M IN HERE MARY!" She opened the car door and said loudly, "We're going to be late for church!" Gus shooed Damian along and hurried towards her beckoning call.

Father Piercy was up on the top of the church steps when he noticed a flashy red beacon coming towards him. Up the church steps, they climbed, until the red cassocked boy stood in front of the priest, and proudly greeted him with, "Salve, Father Jim." Not understanding or hearing Peter correctly, Damian interjected, "No Peter, you're not Father Jim's slave because you're an altar boy!"

Father Jim smiled and said, "You don't understand Damian. He said hello in Latin!" He nodded his head and continued, "Looks like someone is very prepared to join our team of altar boys today."

Mary Malone beamed brightly, as she quickly added, "He was meant to wear those vestments, Father Jim."

The priest smiled, and instructed Damian, "Show Peter around the sacristy and introduce him to the rest of the altar boys, before mass begins." At the bottom of the steps, Damian grinned at his brother, and said, "Come with me, Father Peter…We'll go meet the boys."

On the back of the church, through a separate door, they entered a sacristy full of sarcasm. Inside the boys were jeering and teasing each other, out of the sight from the rest of the congregation. If they weren't whipping each other with the cords of their cassocks, they were kicking each other, when someone turned their back. Young Peter appeared to be in shock, as he watched the chaotic scene unfold before his eyes, in such a holy place. From the corner of the sacristy the older altar boy, called Junior, caught the sight of Peter behind Damian's back. Snapping his cassock cord in the air, he said, "Behold brothers…Damian's holy brother!" With another snap from the cord, he added, "Or should we call him Father Peter…" And with the sarcastic introduction, came a round of laughter from all corners of the room, until Damian replied, "You'll call him Peter, or you'll deal with me."

"Easy now Damian, you know I was only joking." Pretending to be sincere, Junior continued, "Nobody is going to scourge your holy brother." Believing he had made his point with the smirking faces that surrounded the room, Damian began to show his brother around the sacristy.

First, he showed him the altar boy closets for the storage of the cassocks and then showed him the large storage room for the priest's vestments. Next, he opened the cabinet doors and presented the items used for the various types of services, which included everything from baptism to funerals. After that, he pointed towards two additional doors, and said, "That one goes to the altar and that one goes to hell…" With a burst of laughter from the boys getting prepared for mass, Damian jokingly explained, "That's where old statues and relics go to die my brother." From the look on Peter's blank face, Junior added to the conversation with a serious tone, "And it's where they bury old priests, who cross the line with altar boys." The sacristy filled with uncontrollable laugher, until Father Piercy walked through the altar door and asked, "Are you boys ready?" The red cassocked boys and the green cloaked priest quickly lined up before the altar door, then the older altar boy, Junior Landon, turned to Damian with a sly smirk, and mumbled, "Show time…"

Mary Malone was beside herself, when young Peter stepped onto the altar upon a cloud of smoke. Wearing his crisp red cassock and white surplice, he was the only altar boy in perfect formation and folding his hands in proper reverence. As they paraded in front of the foggy congregation, Mrs. Malone blessed herself and looked up to the cloudy ceiling with thankful bliss.

Father Jim began the service with a sharp stare towards the smoking source. In an exaggerated state of numbness, Damian had over swung the thurible until an excessive cloud of smoky incense had filled every church pew. The bellowing incense smoke had the congregation coughing and wheezing out of control, until Father Jim looked at Damian and sliced his hand over the front of his throat, giving the stop signal.

As the smoke rose above the crowd, Father Jim performed the mass rituals with exact perfection. Even the choir noticed there was an extra zip to his tone when he joined in on key without missing a beat. The homily and the passing out of hosts were in perfect harmony with one of the best services Father Jim ever had. He was on his game and everyone in the church clearly knew why, when the Latin was read throughout the mass. Normally, during the past services, Father Jim would say his part in Latin, followed by an undefined mouthful of mumbling from the altar boys. Now, for the first time, Father Jim had a full clear response from the newest altar boy on the block. Mary Malone had taught Peter the Latin parts of the mass over the last year and with this new day, he wasn't holding anything back.

When the church service ended, with blessing of the congregation, Father Jim expressed his feelings of satisfaction to Gus and Mary at the back of the church. While they spoke, Gus caught the attention of his son Damian, and said, "You'll have to leave right away, I need help with the firewood before it rains."

"I'll tell Peter."

"No, leave him here to help the other altar boys."

"But Pop, he's new, and the boys can be pretty mean with new guys."

"They're altar boys! What can they do to hurt him?"

Damian knew they appeared meek from the pews of the church, but behind in the back of the sacristy, they were bold as brass. With Gus Malone pushing him on, there was no time to give caution to Peter, or the warnings to his cocky colleagues. Damian had to do what he was told without question and leave immediately, without the ability to watch over his little brother.

In the sacristy, the boys were busy putting away vestments and candles, until altar boy Junior Landon, noticed Father Jim had left the building. Slowly winking at his fellow altar boys, he slid over in front of Peter and sarcastically said, "What a show you put on, Peter!"

"What do you mean?"

"And that perfect Latin…It was great!"

"My mom taught me."

"Well, you're going to do fine here, Master Peter, just fine."

Looking over at the rest of the boys, Junior softly tapped young Peter on the back and said, "Damian forgot to show you the furnace room…And everyone, should know everything about this place." Pointing towards the door to hell, he continued, "Let's go down for a quick peek…" Peter hesitated when Junior pointed towards the door, but with such friendly persuasion, he followed Junior through the door and down the squeaky steps.

Down below, the dark furnace room was just as creepy as Peter had imagined. Under the light of one hanging lightbulb, he noticed the dirt floor with humps and mounds. In front of the furnace, there was a space surrounded by an army of full-sized statues, which included Saint Kevin and Saint Francis. There were old mass brass relics strewn around and chalices of all types that found peace among the silent statues. All in all, it was not a place where anyone would want to spend one more second, unless they were forced to.

As Peter surveyed the scary surroundings, all the rest of the boys trickled down the stairs until they were standing behind the older altar boy. The trap had been baited and now with a quick nod from the older instigator, the boys grabbed on to young Peter's arms. Junior grabbed a rope from behind the furnace and said, "Now Peter, let's see if your Latin can get you out of this one." They swiftly grabbed on to an old spinning wheel that was used for parish garden parties, and quickly lashed poor Peter on to it. With a rag ready to put into his mouth, Junior said, "This is your penance for showing off with that fancy Latin." But before the rag was rammed in, another boy suggested, "Wait…Why don't you leave the rag out?"

Junior stood down and said, "Explain yourself, or you'll end up on the wheel too."

"Well look around! These guys will watch over him, and if he hollers, they'll come to life and bury him alive." Junior looked at the surrounding statues, and replied, in his most haunting voice, "Yes, they'll bury him with the other priests right below our feet...If he makes one peep." With a quick spin of the wheel, they bounded upstairs and left him spinning under the watchful glare of his ceramic friends.

Back at the Malone home, Damian and his father had flicked all the firewood chunks under the dry safety of the shed. Noticing the job went faster than he expected, Gus asked, "What's got into you boy? You never worked that fast before?" Damian shrugged his shoulders and replied, "Got to help somebody else today."

Gus knew he was up to something, but closed the shed door and said, "Better get going then..."

Damian knew the other altar boys well enough to know, he couldn't trust them with an altar boy who could speak perfect Latin. As he hurried along, he didn't meet Peter on the road, but he could see a small light coming from the basement of the church. Without the return of Peter at home, and with the glow from the basement to hell, Damian quickly understood exactly where his brother Peter could be found.

In the dim light of the dangling light bulb and the low glow from the furnace fire, young Peter had closed his eyes in prayer. Unlike what the other altar boys thought, he was at peace surrounded by the watchful eyes of ceramic saints. Peter was fully accustomed to all sorts of statues, which were positioned all over the Malone household. From the table in the hall, to the night tables in each bedroom, there was plenty of ceramic saints peppered throughout their holy house. Peter was not afraid, as he peacefully waited for a sign of help from up above.

It wasn't long after, Damian descended down the stairs and stopped in disbelief looking at a disgusting site. Even for Damian, this hazing went too far for comfort. The boys had stooped to a new low, and now someone would pay the price for taking a chance with his brother on the spinning wheel. With a calm voice, Peter greeted his brother, "Hi Damian."

Damian quickly grabbed the ropes and said, "Those pricks will pay for this!"

"I'm okay, there's nothing to worry about…"

"It's the point of it, Peter! I'm a senior altar boy, and they didn't respect my brother."

"Let's forget about this, Damian."

"I'll forget nothing, till those pricks pay the price."

The following Saturday, Mrs. Malone was baking bread in the oven, when Damian smelled a brilliant idea. He went to Peter and suggested, "Why don't you ask Mom to cook some muffins for the altar boys. It would be a show of peace and it would keep them off your back." Peter's eyes lit up at the thought of such a nice gesture. He quickly went out to the kitchen and presented the muffin proposal to his mother. Of course, she obliged and went right to work and greased her pans.

Later that night, when the muffins were cooling upon the table, Damian snuck into kitchen and slipped small pieces of chocolate laxative in each muffin. He counted the muffins and made sure there was one for each altar boy and no more. The rest were placed in a bag for his own personal consumption later that night. If all went well, Sunday service for the altar boys would include a treat that would have them running for joy.

Peter picked up the muffins in the morning before Sunday service, and said, "I don't remember Mom putting chocolate chips in these muffins yesterday…And there's two missing…There's none for me and you…"

With nobody left in the house except Damian, he replied, "The only thing matters, is that the boys get a nice treat."

Peter placed them in a paper bag and said, "You were really angry when those boys strapped me to that spinning wheel in the basement, and now you're all about forgiveness." He joined Damian at the door and finished, "You surprise me sometimes, Brother."

Into the sacristy they marched, and politely placed Mary Malone's chocolate chip muffins on the cabinet shelf. Damian stepped up, and said, "Boys, Peter would like to place last week's unfortunate incident behind him. He believes in forgiveness and so, he prepared a little treat for you guys as an offer of peace."

The older altar boy, Junior Landon, was the first to chow down on the chocolate chip muffin, then he was joined by rest of the lads, who were all drooling in anticipation. Shortly after, the tension in the room dissipated with the nice gesture of forgiveness digesting in their stomachs. The priest arrived to find the boys unusually quiet and dressed in their cassocks, ready for action as they marched out through the altar door.

The first sign of trouble came with the twigging and twisting as they started the service. Then came the disturbing sounds of grumbling and rumbling throughout the altar as the mass proceeded through the paces. Later, one by one, each altar boy would grab their stomach and run off the altar and into the sacristy, leaving the priest shorthanded. Damian and Peter continued on to support the mass and the priest, till the final blessing of the congregation.

After mass, when the priest and sick boys had left the sacristy, Peter asked Damian, "What do you suppose happened to the rest of the boys?"

"They're guilty conscious got to them, for putting you on that spinning wheel."

"I hope they'll feel better for next mass."

"Well, if they don't, maybe I'll try some chocolate cake."

"Cake?"

"Never mind…Let's get moving, they'll be expecting us for dinner."

When the boys arrived home for dinner, Mary Malone asked, "What happened to the rest of the altar boys during mass?" Damian never spoke and remained silent while Peter spoke, "They seemed to get sick for some reason. I really don't know why…"

Mrs. Malone sadly said, "They didn't get a chance to eat my fresh muffins." Before another word could be added to the conversation, Damian quickly suggested, "We better get back at that firewood Pop, it won't stack itself…" With Damian's unusual eager approach to firewood, Gus Malone knew something didn't smell right. As soon as Gus and Damian began to store the firewood, he looked at Damian and asked, "What really happened in the sacristy?"

"Just a little pay back Pop, that's all."

"For what?"

"They weren't nice to my brother."

"What did you do boy?"

"Let's just say…It was a shitty situation, Pop."

Gus Malone grinned for one second and then he flicked the firewood upon the stack, and said in a serious tone, "Watch your language boy. If your mother hears you, she'll whip you blind."

Chapter 4

Diminished Candles

On a crisp autumn morning, Gus Malone was unloading firewood from the back of his truck, when Father Piercy's brand new 1970 Dodge Valiant car came tearing in his yard. Through a cloud of dust, the door opened, and Father Piercy's housekeeper Aggie Barrett stumbled out, and cried, "Mr. Malone, Father Jim has fallen…" In seconds flat, Gus was flying back towards the priest's house, with the old housekeeper by his side and the Dodge Valiant's gas pedal right to the floor.

Details had been scanty during the brief ride, but all was crystal clear when he arrived and found his best friend lying on the bathroom floor. Father Jim Piercy was a big jolly man who liked his belly full and his friends close. Now, with no time to waste, Gus Malone picked up the heavy priest like a sack of flour and carried him out into the car with the strength of their forged friendship. Through stop signs of their parish and red lights of the town, Gus kept repeating, "You'll be alright Jim…Just stay with me…" By God's speed and the heavy foot of Gus Malone, Father Jim laid in the hospital bed, opened his eyes, and asked, "What happened Gus?"

"The doctors said you had a small stroke, but you'll be okay."

"How did I get here?"

"Old Mrs. Barrett found you on the floor and drove your car to my place."

"But she never drove before!"

Gus smiled, and said, "She does now…"

Two days had passed with Father Jim Piercy in the hospital, when Gus got a call from his recovering friend. He needed to see him about the parish affairs, and his younger son about something personal. With Peter out in the waiting room, Gus sat by the side of Father Jim as he spoke of his temporary replacement.

"They are sending a temporary priest while I recover."

"Not to worry Jim, we'll take good care of him."

Father Jim sat up in bed and explained, "He's not like some of us, Gus…"

"That's okay Jim, not all priests are perfect like you." With a short smile between the men, Father Jim continued with his eye lids opened to full capacity, "Let's say, he may be leaning towards the other side…" Gus Malone opened his eye lids to duplicate Father Jim, and replied, "Oh…I see." With a shake of the head, Gus continued, "I thought that behavior was looked down upon, from the men of the cloth."

"Well, these days anything goes…After all, it is the seventy's." Father Jim, became serious, and said, "Gus, I don't care what someone's sexual orientation is, I believe in the quality of the person…And this person is a good man and a good priest." Gus Malone looked at his good friend, and said, "If you say he's good, then that's good enough for me." Father Jim looked at his best friend, and said, "I knew I could count on you." Then he asked, "Can you send Peter in?"

Gus Malone gently tapped his old friend on the arm, and said, "Of course."

Peter walked slowly into the room and stood at the end of the hospital bed while he stared at Father Piercy.

"Sit down Peter and let's have a chat."

"Bless me father for I have sinned, it's been a week since I…"

"No, no, my son, you're not here to confess sins. I just want to talk, that's all. Just a little chat…" Father Piercy placed his hand on the bed and said, "Have a seat." Peter sat on the foot of the bed and Father Piercy began. "Peter, you're a good boy…and you have a good heart." He cleared his throat and continued, "I know you're heading for the priesthood, but I want to tell you something before you get too far into the process." Peter was sitting on the bed and listening to Father Jim's every word. He innocently looked at his priest and said, "I'll go all the way, Father."

"I know you can Peter, but I'm asking you to consider your own feelings."

"But Father, shouldn't I consider the feelings of others?"

"Yes, but sometimes, with life decisions, one must consider only themselves."

"I don't understand, Father…"

Lying in the hospital bed looking the heart machine, Father Jim Piercy wanted to get it off his conscience. He finally came straight out and said, "Peter, don't enter the priesthood for others. Follow your own path in life. Do what is good for you."

Without crossing the line of pointing out his mother, Father Piercy had left young Peter with the philosophy of truth, in which he had always believed in. With a clear conscience, Father Jim laid back on the bed and rested, with the thought he had given Peter his true feelings.

On the following Sunday, the church service began with a new priest who had no trouble telling the truth. Father Andrew Truman had taken his sermon over the top and had pushed the envelope with his temporary parishioners to the brink of anarchy. It only took five minutes at the pulpit, before a sense of misunderstanding and confusion began to surface among the crowd. With a clear conscience and crisp voice, Father Andrew had begun, "What if God was gay…"

From every pew the discontent could be tasted in the air, as they twisted and turned to one another, in hopes building the mutual courage of protest. After the word gay had entered the building, all other words were struck down with a wave of mumblings until the words crested and finally broke. From each corner of the church, one by one the comments came. "That's sacrilegious!" And kept coming, "God forgive you…" It all came to a stormy halt, when Gus Malone stood to his feet and shouted, "Enough!"

Father Andrew Truman was ready to throw in the good book, until Gus Malone surprisingly spoke on his behalf. Gus looked at his fellow friends and family, then said, "Give this man a chance to finish." With full attention captured from everyone, he continued, "If Father Jim believes in him, we must hear him out." Gus sat back down in a pin-drop silence, while Father Andrew cleared his throat, and explained, "It was meant to be hypothetical…I'm just asking, what difference does it mean? Would you treat God any different?"

The priest continued on with his sermon, and by the end of it, his sincere level of humanity had struck a nerve of understanding with everyone in the church. In fact, as the weeks went by, Father Andrew's sincere sermons became accepted and expected with each passing Sunday mass. In the end, Gus's devout friend had not steered him in the wrong direction with the new priest's quality of character.

As time carried on, what appeared to be a temporary time with Father Andrew, turned out to be longer than expected by the spiraling decline of Gus's old friend. Late one night, the phone rang, causing Gus Malone to close his eyes in prayer while he reluctantly picked up the receiver. The recent visits to the hospital had been very unsettling for Gus, with Father Jim's rapid loss of knowledge. Gus and Father Jim were best friends, and now his friend didn't know who he was, or where he came from. Gus had watched every day, as the once sharp minded man began to have difficulty with the simple tasks. It was clear to him, the sparkle in his friend's light blue eyes had finally faded to dull black. With the expected news from the hospital, Gus placed the phone down with relief, and thanked God, his best friend had passed away.

After the final send off for Father Piercy, the Archdiocese changed Father Andrew Truman's temporary assignment into a permanent position. He became a full parish Priest under the watchful eyes of Mary Malone, who had the ear of her cousin Father Tom Burns. If the modern priest strayed from their strict agenda, it would be relayed to the Archdiocese without delay.

The intensity of Father Truman did not falter or fail to disappoint the faint of heart. He continued to fan the flame of hot topics, until he fired-up Mary Malone and her cousin Tom Burns to the point of internal combustion. From women's rights to gay rights and every other right that was wrong, Father Truman did not stand down, until Bishop Stone paid him a visit at the invitation of Mary Malone and Tom Burns.

The Archdiocese had heard enough ambiguous rantings, and it was time to lay down the cardinal law with clear conviction. One renegade priest was out of control and it was high time the high priest, Bishop Stone, finally put him back in his place. The decision was made, and Father Truman's loose tongue would be silenced with a stiff tongue whipping in front of his parish.

As planned, on the following Sunday Bishop Stone appeared to all, wearing his high hat and full formal dress. The mass went smoothly along, with everything working in perfect order, as they went mechanically through the motions. Bishop Stone even seemed extra pleased with altar boy Peter Malone's clear Latin lingo during their celebration of mass. All appeared to be in peaceful order, until the end of the mass and the Bishop walked to the pulpit.

Bishop Stone's stern face gave a glimpse of what had been expected by Mary Malone. She was assured that things would be different, from her frank conversations with Father Burns. The Bishop slipped around the pulpit, pointed directly at Father Andrew, and began, "It has been reported…that Father Truman has deviated from a path laid out by the Holy See." With Mary Malone's head nodding in agreement from the front pew, the Bishop continued, "We do not support it…and we will not tolerate it in any way, shape or form." Once again, he received nodding support from the front ranks of the pews and once again he continued with his skinny finger in the face of Father Truman, "This man will be punished for his mistakes and we…" Before another word was muttered from his mouth, a strong voice bellowed from the back of the church and asked, "WHO…do you THINK…you ARE?"

In the last pew, Gus Malone stood with his finger pointing towards the shrinking Bishop. With the attention of the congregation captured, he continued in a loud voice, "You have no right to chastise this good man…He has spoken nothing but the truth…" The Bishop walked behind the pulpit and Gus pointed out, "You come here with your high hat and big way, but he sits there as a humble man with an honest heart." Gus Malone looked at his fellow parishioners and asked, "Who really, has deviated from the path of God?"

There were no additional discussions, debates, or even disparaging remarks that degraded Father Andrew Truman. Bishop Stone didn't even stay for a lovely dinner, that housekeeper Aggie Barrett had thoughtfully prepared. There was no fanfare for red faced Bishop Stone. He was in his plush seat and gone, leaving nothing but crushed stone, flying from the tires of his shiny black car.

After supper that evening, Gus took the wet pot from Mary to dry, and said, "Seems to me, someone may have complained to the Bishop." Mary Malone slowly kept washing the remaining pots without comment. Gus continued to dry the pots, and said, "It's a pity we all don't see what's really important."

Mary dropped one of the pans in sink, turned to face her husband and exclaimed, "Don't you see Gus, Father Andrew has everything wrong!"

Gus Malone threw the towel towards the table in disgust, and replied, "I can see…some are blinded by the glory of power."

Mary continued to wash her pans, and replied, "We have Peter's position to think about…"

Gus opened the door to walk outside and said, "He would learn more truth from Father Andrew than any of those high and mighty priests from the Archdiocese." With a slam of the door, Gus walked on, knowing for a short period, Peter would be in safe hands with their good priest Father Andrew Truman.

There was an eerie silence from the Bishop, as the Sunday mass ritual continued without retaliation. As time moved away from the attempted chastising, Father Andrew became a close mentor to the young boy who was quickly moving towards his predetermined holy path. Plenty of conversations of religion and theology filled the sacristy, before and after each mass. Peter was becoming more enlighten with every passing day, but Father Andrew sensed something was amiss from time to time. After getting to know his parents quite well, Father Andrew suspected the trouble could be related to Mary Malone's personal push for Peter's religious redemption.

At the end of regular mass, before they sat down and had their usual conversation in the sacristy, Father Andrew addressed his suspicions with Peter. He placed his vestment in the closet, and said, "You know Peter, it's great to have such a lofty goal as the priesthood."

"I believe it's my destiny, Father…"

"Is it, Peter?"

"Isn't, Father?"

"I really don't know about that Peter, but what I do know is…your destiny must be yours and not someone else's."

"Are you suggesting it's my mother's destiny?"

"What I'm trying to tell you…is…you have to take your own path in life."

"Father Andrew, I truly want to be a priest."

Father Andrew smiled, looked into his eyes, sincerely and said, "You will make the best priest someday…"

One year on and many conversations later, Peter was still pursuing his holy path and Father Andrew had continued to hold nothing back at the pulpit. With each Sunday mass, the bar for controversial topics was lowered, while the fear of retribution from the Archdiocese increased. It had appeared the holy order was keeping away from the controversial priest, until one morning his housekeeper handed him a letter from the Archdiocese.

Later on, during one of their conversations about pros and cons of the priesthood, Father Truman found the right time to say, "It is time for me to go."

"But we've been only talking for a short while."

"No, I mean leave this parish for good."

"But why?"

"I received notification from the Archdiocese."

"But you've only been here a short while…"

"I don't think it's a secret that I don't see eye to eye with the Archdiocese."

"To what parish will they send you?"

"According to the letter, they are sending me far from here…"

"But you're a good priest, Father Andrew."

"Thank you, my son, that means more than you would know."

Father Andrew was never a true believer in the mysterious ways of the Archdiocese. He didn't know exactly what was going on, but he did understand something wasn't right behind those closed walls. Faced with a letter that forced him away from a good parish and a stable life, Father Andrew was not concerned for himself. He was however, very concerned that Peter's priestly path could place him in harm's way, and he would not be there to protect him. Father Andrew looked at the disappointment on Peter's face and said, "On your journey of life, don't place all your trust in men…You will be disappointed."

"But who do I place my trust in, if not mankind?"

"Place your trust in yourself…and God!"

Father Andrew was not positive if Peter's priesthood dream belonged to him or someone else. He only knew for sure, that Peter Malone was headed straight into a dark place, because there was a bad wind blowing through the holy halls of the Archdiocese.

Chapter 5

Bad Wind Blows

The word from the Archdioceses was final and the action they took was swift. This time there would be no wavering or wondering in the plain view of parishioners, where discontent could be mounted. Bishop Stone would not put himself in harm's way on unfamiliar ground or in front of clear voices of reason. From beneath the pretense of the almighty, and under the auspicious of the Holy Archdioceses, Bishop Stone would flex his muscle with the parish appointment of Father McKnight.

In the arms of the leather-bound chairs of Archdiocese, Bishop Stone poured out a single malt scotch, gave it to the replacement priest, and said, "Remember, we will not tolerate and further pushback or unwillingness." With a clink of the glass, Father McKnight replied, "Of course your Excellency."

"We need to show them, who is boss."

"Indeed, your Excellency…"

"We need to send a clear message…"

With another clink of the glass, Father McKnight replied, "Leave it to me your Excellency, they'll see who's in charge…real fast."

At the crack of dawn, when the sun began to rise over the parish, the evidence of change was in the open for everyone to see. Father McKnight had initiated his intention of sending a strong message on who was in charge. There was nothing left standing, to leave a doubt or question on how the parish would be ruled from that day on. With every beautiful tree and each bush cut to the ground, the message was crystal clear for all parishioners. There was a new priest in town, and it was time to play by the rules of the Archdiocese, or consequences would be felt from the long arm of Bishop Stone.

On Sunday, the people of the parish filed into the church and filled the pews with heavy hearts. Their beautiful lush church garden of tall trees and bushy shrubs was a peaceful testament to the love they expressed for their parish and church. Trimmed by hand with meticulous care, the manicured garden paradise was a place to rest their weary souls and pray under the cool shadow of its protecting branches. Without conversation or consideration, it had been returned to dust, to show the power of the pulpit. Father McKnight had made his point loud and clear, with the leveling of their paradise garden and his long sermon of fire and brimstone.

Behind the scenes, the changing of the guard was in full process for the altar boys. It was Damian's last year in service of the altar, and he was only too glad to the end of his unwilling participation. He had played his part for Mary Malone but now it was time to take his final bow upon the altar. If Damian played his cards right and kept his nose clean, time would not fence him in for too much longer.

For Peter, the time remaining was embraced with open arms. Although the long discussions of faith, with his friend Father Andrew were gone, he was still satisfied to serve at the feet of any holy servant. With his sharp Latin and his sharply pressed cassock, he would shine in the eyes of the heavy-handed priest in the presence of his vigilant mother.

At the delight of Father McKnight, three new fresh-faced altar boys were also on hand to welcome his dark reign of fear and suspicion. Kevin Callum, Mark Godfrey and Justin Morey stood arm to arm with each other, as the new priest inspected their every move. While Father McKnight scowled at the sight of his older altar boys with head-strong ideas, he smiled at the newly minted altar boys with their weak dispositions. With his blatant body language, Damian could easily see, that the new priest desired bridled young bucks, who could be molded into obedience.

At the Malone household, Gus was not pleased with the loss of their beautiful church garden or the site of their new militant priest. Gus's gut was also telling him, there was something dark about the priest that he couldn't see. This was confirmed, when his older son returned home and shone the light upon his suspicion. In the privacy of the shed, Damian blurted out, "I don't like that new priest Pop…"

"Why do you say that, son?"

"He's creepy, that's all."

"That's not much to go on, son."

"He was acting too weird with the new altar boys."

"I don't like the sound of that, boy…"

"I didn't like the sight of it, Pop."

Gus Maloney looked through the window and replied, "We'll have to keep a close on that guy, Damian."

During the next few weeks, Damian watched the comings and goings of Father McKnight's odd behavior. He noticed, every other night two priests would join Father McKnight's parish priest house and would not leave till the late hours of the morning. He watched the cases of booze carried in by Father McKnight's two friends, Father Blake and Father Sable. From his diligent surveillance, he understood by the long face of housekeeper Aggie Barrett, all was not right in the parish's holy house.

As the close watch continued, Father McKnight suspected he was under suspicion from Damian's watchful glare. Each close encounter with the young altar boys and every late night, was acknowledged from a distance by Damian. However, his close quarter glances were not gone without notice. The dark priest had seen Damian watching from the shadows very clearly and had a plan in place to end the secret surveillance.

Father McKnight was well aware, that the thin-tasting communion wine didn't align with its expensive label. He also knew the oldest altar boy was the cause of his missing wine. Although he understood quite well who the perpetrator was, he had a bigger plan in place before he would take the perfect pounce.

Altar boy Junior Landon was in the sacristy pouring the wine, when Damian came in and warned, "You're going to get caught."

"If I was stupid like you Damian, I would…"

"McKnight is on to you Landon."

"You don't know shit, Malone…"

"I know he's watching your shit head."

Junior took a guzzle from the bottle and then filled it to the top with water, shook it and offered it to Damian, "Here…just take a swig, and then fill it with water. That stupid holy asshole would never know the difference." Damian took the bottle to place back in the cupboard, when Father McKnight quickly opened the basement door said, "Well…well…what do we have here?"

It was no coincidence that Father McKnight was lurking in the basement with his ear to the door. He was a seasoned drinker and knew the wine had been turned to water, by the hand of an altar boy. Although he understood exactly which altar boy performed the diluting miracle, he had waited until the right time to blame the wrong boy.

Damian was not the type to tell on anyone, no matter what he really felt about that person. He stood with the bottle in his hand, and said, "I have the wine ready for service Father." Father McKnight walked toward Damian with a fake smile, and sarcastically said, "Indeed you do…" Without warning, he seized the watered wine from his hand and slapped his face as hard as he could. With spit flowing from his red face, he said, "Get your sealing soul out of my sacristy!"

Damian, grabbed his coat and stormed through the door with only one thought in mind. He could only think about the safety of his brother and the innocent naive altar boys left behind. He knew very well, they were left to holy wolves, without anyone there to watch the innocent flock in the shadow of the sacristy.

Damian arrived home and didn't get two steps into the kitchen, when he came face to face with his mother. Father McKnight had called ahead to ensure his faith was sealed with Mary Malone, who was standing in the doorway with a distant stare. Gus was not aware and had no idea, that his young spy would receive the bony back of the hand for the second time that day. With the shouting from Mary Malone and the loud slap, echoing off the walls, it was too late to defend his valiant warrior.

Unprotected, and without further distractions, the safety of the sacristy began to unravel for the altar boys, with Father McKnight's introduction to his two cloaked friends. The false sense of security that came from white collars and black cloaks, allowed them to take their trust and breach an innocent world. With their guards down, one young boy from a broken family, became caught in a despicable trap. Kevin Callum was alone and unaware of the danger, when Father Sable offered to drive him home after mass.

A ride that only should have taken ten minutes, seemed eternity to the small victim. During that fall evening, when the sun retreated early, one little boy's light had been taken under the cloak of darkness. Unaware of what had happened, that small fragile child had seen the darkest side of humanity. Under the dark hands of hell, thirty minutes had come and gone, with the opening of a big black door and the closing of innocence, for young Kevin Callum.

The next day, Peter Malone was passing the playground and spotted young Kevin sitting on a silent swing. He walked over, sat on the other swing, and asked, "Are you going to the sacristy this afternoon?" Without a response,

Peter continued, "They will be preparing for the thanksgiving celebration, if you interested in helping."

The little boy stared into space and questioned Peter in a soft voice, "Where did the angels go, when I wanted them?" Peter shifted in the seat without replying. He didn't know the whereabouts of angels, or why they didn't come. Small tears began to drip from the boy's cheeks, while he whispered, "Why was I alone Peter?" Again, poor Peter wasn't equipped for the question or Kevin's lonely concerns. The innocent child wept uncontrollably into his small hands, looked up at Peter's blank face, and asked, "Where did the love of God go, when I needed him?"

One crow landed upon a nearby post, and silently watched as the silence grew between the two boys. On that somber day, there were no answers to be found in the playground. Two young kids weren't prepared to answer something they couldn't understand. Young Peter Malone was oblivious to the reality of the details and little Kevin Callum was too traumatized by the transgression of the evil priest. Full of frustration, Kevin dropped to pick up a rock. He looked at the crow, threw it in the opposite direction, and angrily said, "I don't want to be an altar boy anymore…" The black crow cawed and lifted to the open sky, where only the angels of mercy knew the answer of what really had happened, under the eyes of God.

The previous day Damian had been up on Mill Road to check on his Father's firewood and had seen Father Sable with little Kevin Callum. He did not see the despicable deed or know for sure something had occurred on that empty road. He only knew that the sight of Father Sable with the young boy in that lonely place, had left a dark forbidding shadow in the crease of his mind. Knowing very well, that the reporting back with unfounded accusations may place him in harm's way, he decided to confide in the only person he could count on.

Damian peeped through the shed window and saw his Father shaping a piece of wood for a chair he had just carved from scratch. Gus Malone was a top-notch carpenter and did things the old-fashioned way with sweat of his brow and care in his heart. There would be no short cuts taken for Gus Malone, if it would compromise the quality of his work or his life. Like the real timber he held in his rough hands, Gus Malone was true to the core and strong in mind. Damian knew he could lean on him without bending the alarm or sending out unnecessary mixed messages.

"What's up boy? Why the gloomy face?"

"I don't know how to say it, Pop…"

"Just spit it out, son."

"I saw Father McKnight's priest friend with little Kevin Callum."

"I don't like it, but that's not unusual son."

"He was down on Mill Road yesterday evening with Kevin…alone."

"We have a big problem on our hands boy…big problem…"

"What are we going to do, Pop?"

Gus Malone put the old wood plane down, scratched his head, and said, "You're going back on the altar…"

"But, Pop…they'll slap the face off me for trying…"

"Not if I'm there, with truth in my hands."

Gus Malone had been told the story of wine to water by Damian and believed every word. He also knew the altar boy Junior Landon's father very well and hoped he would help him set the record straight. If he could get Bill Landon's ear, in front of both boys, maybe the truth would come out under the pressure of honest men. Gus opened the shed door and signaled with the shift of his head, "Let's go for little ride, son."

On the outside of the parish, far from the grasp of the church, an old house leaned against the cold wind. From the absence of paint and the loss of roof shingles, it would be difficult to believe someone would be living under that leaky roof. As Gus Malone pulled up in front of the haggard home, Damian said disgustingly, "I didn't realize Junior lived like this." Gus looked at his son, and said, "Don't judge people by the walls that surround them son. At any time, the walls can tumble in on anyone."

Bill Landon had lost everything that meant anything to him. Bill's wife had suffered a long bout of cancer and died in the embrace of his arms. His two daughters had tragically passed away a few years earlier, under the wheels of a drunk driver. He had lost his way with both tragedies and found the only remedy that could ease the pain, was at the bottom of a bottle. Bill Landon had been battered in life by the loss of his beloved wife and daughters, but through it all, Gus Malone knew, Bill's integrity remained intact.

Gus walked confidently on to the step with Damian by his side. The squeaky door opened and as Bill stepped outside, Gus greeted him with a simple, "Hello Bill."

"Gus."

"Mind if we talk a bit?"

"Come in…"

The room was surprisingly clean, for a widower with one young son. It was hard to miss the family pictures of lost loves ones, which Bill hung on every hook and placed on every table. For a moment, Gus was lost in thought, wondering if they were watching over floors that once carried the weight of laughter and tears. He was quickly brought back to his senses when Bill asked, "What's this about, Gus?"

"There was an incident with your boy in the sacristy of the church."

Bill had signed young Junior up to be an altar boy when his wife had died. He was not a church goer but knew his wife's love for the church and everything it represented. Out of respect for his wife and in hopes it would keep his son straight, Bill Landon placed him in the safety of the church. Bill was not a man of many words, but he was a straight shooter who didn't mess around. He quickly said in a loud voice, "Junior…Get out here…"

Young Junior didn't hesitate to quickly come into the living room and didn't stop on saying, "I told that prick, it wasn't Damian's fault."

Bill Landon looked sternly at his son and asked, "Well tell us what happen…"

Young Junior looked over at Damian, and said, "When he slapped you and you ran out, I told him, he made a mistake…I told him…it was me who drank his friggn' wine."

"What did he say?"

"He told me to shut my mouth or he'd ram the bottle down it." Like his father Bill Landon, young Junior may have been rough at times, but he never lied at any time. Bill

Landon quickly stood up and exclaimed, "I'll ram my fist down his god dammed throat…"

"Easy Bill…we're working on something."

"How can I help Gus?" Gus Malone shook Bill's hand and said, "We'll have to get Damian back on the altar, where he can watch his every move." Bill nodded his head and suggested, "Take the boy with you."

As they drove up to the priest's house, Damian whispered to Junior, "Do you still steal the wine?" Junior grinned and replied in a low voice, "Nah…I don't drink it, but I taste it." Puzzled by his answer, he asked, "How do manage that?" Junior leaned towards Damian and whispered, "I gargle the wine it in my mouth and spits it back in the bottle." Damian laughed, leaned towards Junior, and whispered, "Serves the prick right…"

After knocking loudly on the door and waiting longer that anyone should, housekeeper Aggie Barrett finally opened the door a few inches and asked abruptly, "What do you want?"

"We need to speak to the priest."

"What about?"

"That's none of your business…"

Gus was about to lose his patience, until Father McKnight appeared and said, "Now, now…no need to get cranky between friends…"

"Sorry for the late intrusion, but we need to clear up an urgent matter."

Father McKnight stared at Damian by the side of his father, glanced over at Junior on the other side and asked, "Can it wait until a more suitable hour of the day?" Junior Landon stepped forward and said, "Like I told you before,

Father, it was me who drank the wine and not Damian…"
Father McKnight took one step back to consider matters,
then one step ahead and asked, "Can't an honest priest make
a simple mistake?" With his obvious confession, the
slippery priest avoided any further interrogation from his
three feisty guests. He quickly said to Damian without an
apology, "I'll see you back on the altar on Sunday." Then
he turned to Junior. "You, my boy, I will not." Young Junior
Landon smiled, and with a nod of his head, he said, "You
can work that wine bottle up your ass…"

With such high stakes, Gus was not worried about flak
from his wife for recruiting Junior Landon. He knew very
well that Father McKnight would fill in the blanks, before
they backed out from the driveway. As they drove home
Damian asked, "What do you think Mom will do?"

"She'll carry on as if nothing happened son…"

"My swollen face tells me, something happened."

Gus Malone hauled up into their driveway, and said, "A
slap in the face will be a small price to pay, if we can keep
Peter and those young kids away from the clutches of Father
McKnight."

Chapter 6

Fallen Angel

As autumn turned to winter, Mill Road became a memory for most, while their minds filled with Christmas preparations. Without any sound evidence or the voice of little Kevin Callum, the unspoken story of Mill Road lay in a limbo of silence. But as time moved on and most memories had faded, one boy did not forget the murky incident on Mill Road. While the wine flowed freely and the scotch kept pouring, Damian continued to watch, while the three fallen priests came and went under the light of the full moon.

It appeared, the presence of Damian on the altar had pushed the wolves back into their den of iniquity and away from the lure of the innocent lambs. In reality, they knew an opportunity would open, and it would only be a matter of time before Damian would fall into another trap. Unfortunately, as Christmas Eve drew near, there was no need for anymore priestly scheming. On his own accord, Damian gave them an unexpected gift, unwrapped and blowing in the wind.

At the Malones, Christmas wouldn't be the same without the traditional meal of fish followed by a trip to church for Midnight Mass. It was something they all looked forward to, and this year seemed be no exception until pasty faced Damian sat down to a full plate of fish. With everyone else forking into the fish, Damian pushed it around the plate without eating a bite. Mary Malone noticed the untouched fish and demanded, "You better eat that fish, Damian."

"But Mom, I'm not feeling well."

"I don't care what you're feeling, you are going to eat it, or wear it."

Not aware of the severity of his sick stomach, Gus waded into the conversation, and suggested, "Eat your fish boy."

"But, Pop…"

"Try and eat some…"

Bite by bite, Damian slowly forced the fish food into his grumbling stomach, until he reached the halfway point. Mrs. Malone was watching intensely and began to grab the plate to force the situation, when Gus said, "The boy has had enough."

The boys made it down to the sacristy early, in order to prepare for the Christmas Eve mass. It was an extra special mass that required plenty of candles and other time-consuming preparations. In the middle of a busy sacristy, with altar boys coming and going, nobody missed Damian going down into the furnace room holding on to his sore stomach.

Down below in the basement, the furnace had not engaged the blower to heat the interior of the church. This was normal, as the furnace was old and from time to time it would not operate, even in the coldest days. In the silence of the basement, poor Damian could not hold the stomach pain one second longer. He squeezed between the furnace, held on to the ducting, and let it all go. He believed that later, when it was safe to do so, he would clean up his mess at another time. After all, it was very unusual for anyone to be down in the basement of the church, at any time of year. With the pressure relieved, a lighter Damian returned upstairs as fast as he could, where the air was cool and clean.

The boys quickly lined up in the sacristy and with a quick cough from the Priest they entered the nave, where the congregation was waiting with opened arms in the cold pews. In standing room only, the packed church of parishioners huddled together for warmth, while the old furnace remained silent.

Father McKnight did not wait for the faltering furnace to start blowing out the heat. He had plans to meet with his midnight friends later and did not want to miss the pouring of Christmas scotch. As the mass carried on, the warmth from the tightly packed crowd eased the bitter sting of the biting cold. Without procrastinating, the priest stood up to the pulpit and began his regular sermon of fire and brimstone. While sparks from his heavy-handed words came flying freely from his red face, the lights dimmed for a second and then the flow of furnace air began. Standing in front of the pulpit, the priest pointed upwards, and said, "Ah…I see someone up above is listening to my sermon on this glorious occasion…"

In a normally solemn mass held by Father McKnight, there was a brief hint of smiles that was tolerated by the typically strict priest. The smug grin on his face showed everyone attending mass, that the magnitude of his furnace miracle permitted a brief display of warmth. As the warm air continued to blow into the faces of the crowd, the furnace circulation picked up a fresh source to blow through the ducting. It was then, the smiles changed to frowns as the warm air blasted out through the ducting with a terrible smell.

Down in the nave of the church, there was a continual turn of heads within pews, trying to pinpoint the source of the smell. From the altar to the nave and right on out through the vestibule, the terrible stench had permeated the entire church. In the midst of fire and brimstone, Father McKnight had presented the parish with an unpleasant gift and a Christmas Eve they would never forget.

After a very hasty blessing at the end of mass, they scurried into the sacristy for fresh air. With no ducting in the sacristy and no toilet in the church, Father McKnight remembered the timing of the stench lined up with the miraculous firing of the furnace. He quickly flicked open the basement door and reluctantly headed down into the stinky basement. Holding his nose with one hand, he pointed towards the troubled area and said "That dirty little boy..." He also noticed something that fell out of the perpetrator's pocket. Just to the right of the Damian's dump, lay a small wooden cross that was worn over an altar boy's cassock. Under the light of the dangling bulb, the engraving clearly spelled out DAMIAN. The priest grinned in the middle of the sink, and mumbled to himself, "You just gave me the best Christmas present!"

Father McKnight bounced up over the basement stairs, went right into the face of Damian and exclaimed, "You are a dirty, despicable boy!"

"But Father, I was sick, and there was nowhere to go…"

"Oh…You got somewhere to go all right…"

"I was going to clean it up when everyone left, but…" With his bony finger pointing towards the door, Father McKnight shouted, "GET OUT!"

Damian went straight to the shed without delay and told his Pop about the fallout of the furnace fiasco. Gus Malone looked sternly at his son, and said, "I should have never forced you to eat that fish…It's my fault son…"

"That don't matter, Pop…When Mom finds out, I'm going to be fishmeal."

Knowing his wife would be notified by Father McKnight, Gus looked at the son who had put himself in harm's way for others, and said, "You have taken enough knocks for all us…And you will take no more…"

Mary Malone did come home steaming from the nostrils but quickly tamed down when Gus took control. Without raising his voice in anger, he placed a plan on the table that everyone could understand and accept. Damian would go to live with his uncle in the city, away from the parish and away from the reach of his mother's back hand. On Boxing Day, Gus placed in his son's hand, an envelope of money that he couldn't afford, and said, "Your uncle is a good man and will look after you in the city."

Damian shook his Pop's outstretched hand and said, "Keep a close eye on Peter, he could be in trouble."

"He won't touch Peter under your mother's watch…"

"That priest is sick."

"Yes, he is son…but he's not stupid."

Later that night in the clergy house, when Mary Malone informed Father McKnight of Damian's hasty departure, a toast was offered up to freedom. At last, Father McKnight, Sable and Blake would be free to cull the flock of its innocence. On the cusp of a new year, the corks were popped and the single malt scotch poured freely throughout the night. With a continual clink of the glass, they all knew very well, that one angel had fallen from his vigilant post and was cast out to the far away city.

Back at the Malone's, all was not sitting well for Peter. He had not been included in any discussions about the late-night suspicious behavior of Father McKnight and his two priestly friends. Peter was not aware of the shed conversations between his father and brother that debated the Mill Road incident. He was not told of the false accusations of wine stealing that had been thrown at his brother in a fit of rage by Father McKnight. Peter had been kept from any negative input that would disrupt their dream, by his overprotective mother.

Even though Peter's eyes had been covered by his mother, he could see things that didn't align with his own vision of a holy life. The years had come and gone since the time of Father Piercy, but he did not forget his father's best friend. He remembered Father Jim very well, and all the good deeds he had done for those inside and outside the parish. Peter also thought about his friend, Father Andrew Truman. He remembered all the uncluttered conversations and Father Andrew's honest approach to all and any controversial topics. Both good priests had imprinted a vision of what he had aspired towards as he journeyed towards his lofty goal. Peter may not have been privy to all the dirty details about McKnight and friends, but he understood quite well, that their directive was very different from the good message of Father Jim and Father Andrew.

In the absence of good, Peter decided to leave the altar at the relief of his father and the dismay of his mother. Without giving his mother the full understanding of his misgivings about Father McKnight, Peter stepped down from an altar that he adored. Mary Malone may have been disappointed but Gus Malone was relieved to know that his son was finally out of range from McKnight's grasp. From that point on, seventeen-year-old Peter would make the one-hour trip to attend a mass served by a priest he knew very well.

Father Andrew Truman had been bounced from pillar to post, in all sorts of parishes that were out of sight and out of the Archdiocese's mind. He finally secured a small parish in a remote area, far from the prying eyes of any righteous onlookers. In this place, Father Andrew finally found somewhere where he could freely spread the word of honest truth. Far from the prying eyes of the Archdiocese, Father Andrew received his long-distance friend with open arms and ears. After a refreshing Sunday mass, Peter sat with Father Andrew and said, "It hasn't been the same since you left our parish."

"Every priest has their own way, Peter…"

"I don't like his way at all…"

Father Andrew smiled at Peter and asked, "If you don't like him, I'm sure Damian hates him."

"Damian has left the parish, because of him."

Father shook his head and responded, "That's sad. Damian is a good guy."

Peter nodded and said, "He always had my back…"

"I assume the actions of Father McKnight has changed your plan to enter the priesthood."

"I aspire to you and Father Piercy, not him."

"And your mother, of course…"

Father Andrew stood up and asked, "So you're ready to join us?"

"Not yet, I'm still waiting for a sign…"

Father Andrew struck him playfully on the arm, smiled, and said, "Well, you won't find any sign hanging over us today…I'll see you next Sunday."

The unexpected news of Peter leaving the altar didn't put a frown on Father McKnight's face. Actually, during the final few times Peter was on the altar, Father McKnight seemed more upbeat than ever. His strict demeanor had changed, and he was more casual towards the younger altar boys Mark Godfrey and Justin Morey. While the priest's pleasant attitude continued to bloom among the young boys, the long-distant mass receptions increased Father McKnight's frosty reception towards him. One evening, while picking up personal items he had left in the sacristy, Father McKnight walked in front of Peter and sarcastically said, "Your mother tells me you're hanging around Father Andrew's parish."

"I find his mass enlightening." Peter respectfully replied.

"Maybe you'll find this enlightening…" He couldn't help squirting out a sly smirk, as he continued, "The word at the Archdiocese is…Father Andrew is a gay priest…"

From the first time he saw Father McKnight's smug face after destroying the church garden to last the time he watched him gloat at the banishing of his beloved brother, he did not like him. He also realized how he affected his thoughts of becoming a priest. In a controlled but emotional tone, Peter stared at McKnight, and replied, "I don't know if he's gay or not, and I don't care, but what I do know very clearly…that he's a better priest than you'll ever be…and that's all that matters to me."

Peter left his beloved church and vowed he would never return there while Father McKnight stood behind the pulpit. By that time, he had seen enough strange things and heard enough disturbing stories to know, he would not follow in the footsteps of Father McKnight. If there was any sign sent that would show him the holy way to the altar, it would not be in the company of that distorted priest.

Undaunted on his altered path, Peter continued to travel to mass every Sunday at the church served by his friend Father Andrew Truman. While getting ready to go one morning, his altar-boyfriend, Justin Morey, came to him for help. Young Justin stood at the door and said, "I didn't know who to turn to and what to say…"

Peter walked him over to the bench in their front garden, and assured him, "You came to the right place." They sat down and he asked, "How can I help, Justin?"

"When you left the altar Father Blake and Father Sable took us on a camping trip."

"Where was Father McKnight?"

"I heard, he had business with the Archdiocese."

"What happen? How can I help?"

"Can you have a talk with Mark Godfrey?"

"Why?"

"Something is not right with him, since the camping trip…"

It was no secret between them that Mark Godfrey lived in a poor area of the parish, where he had seen his share of misery. Living on cheques that came from the government coffers, food was scarce, and love was an elusive concept for the Godfrey family. Mark's parents were two lost souls who left their son Mark Godfrey to the whims of nature. He was alone and vulnerable without the guiding hand or the protection of a loving family.

Peter found young Mark down at the local fishing hole, alone and sitting on the edge of an overlooking bank. He passed him a brown paper bag and said, "I thought I'd find you here…"

Without speaking, the young boy quickly opened the bag and wolfed down the first section of the sandwich. Peter threw a rock in the pond while the poor boy swallowed a whole piece and clutched the other section of the sandwich. Watching him through the sides of his eyes, Peter quietly stated, "Justin told me, you're not yourself since the camping trip…"

Young Mark took a slow bite and replied in a spacy tone, "I thought they would have hotdogs at the campfire."

"Did something happen, while you were there?"

It was quickly apparent to Peter that Mark was anywhere but there. He immediately understood by Mark's distant demeanor that putting him somewhere he didn't want to be was going to be a difficult task. Peter tossed another rock softly into the pond, and gently asked, "What happened?"

Mark stared out onto the pond, and said, "The zipper of the tent came open and Father Blake came in…" In a trance, he continued to mumble, "I like marshmallows, Peter. Do you like marshmallows, Peter?"

"Yes, I like them too, Mark."

"We put them on the fire…and after…We had hot chocolate Peter…"

Still in a trance the young boy went silent until Peter softly asked, "What happened then Mark?" The hungry little boy threw the rest of his sandwich in the pond, and finished, "I could hear the zipper of the tent closing."

After that point, Peter only received rambling thoughts that continued in a circle of silence. Through the spaces young Mark left out of the conversation, he knew something bad occurred to a fragile boy, who was an easy victim of circumstances. In the company of Father Blake and Father Sable, another incident of ambiguity had occurred under the blessing of Father McKnight. With no avenue of recourse to question the powerful establishment, Peter journeyed home, with too many nagging questions that came with impossible answers.

Justin Morey was waiting for Peter to return, to make some sort of sense out of Mark Godfrey's strange behavior. Opening the fence gate, Justin quickly asked, "What did you find out?"

"Nothing…"

"Nothing…but something is not right with him."

"Yes…He's hurting but he won't say why…"

"I'm worried about him, Peter."

"I'm worried about all of you guys."

"Well don't worry about me. My dad just got a job as the grounds keeper for the church." Peter smiled, nodded his head in relief, and said, "That's good. Now we'll have someone keeping an eye on Father Sable and Father Blake…" He looked at Justin, and finished, "…and watching out, for you guys too." Knowing that Pat Morey was on duty at the priest's house, Peter finally let his guard down and began to concentrate on the higher call from above.

Chapter 7

Catalyst for Change

Even though Peter Malone was sitting at the back of the church, Father Andrew could plainly see that something was not right with his young friend. Afterwards, when Sunday service was over and they began their regular talk, Father Andrew asked, "Is there something wrong at home?"

"Home is fine, but I fear for the boys at the parish church…"

"I understand you don't like Father McKnight, and I'm certainly not fond of him, but he's not a monster Peter." Peter sighed, looked at Father Andrew straight in the face, and asked, "But, is he?"

"That's a pretty strong suggestion, coming from a person who wants to be a priest."

"You don't understand, there have been many instances where questionable behavior has been seen and heard about his friends, Father Sable and Father Blake."

By the serious look upon Father Andrew's face, Peter knew there was more to the parish's accusations. Of course, Father Andrew could not divulge any inkling of suspicion, under the auspicious of his priestly position. As Peter poured out his heart and stories, all Father Andrew could offer, was a simple, "I see…"

Father Andrew's ambiguous replies continued, until Peter wanted more from his understanding friend. After telling about his conversation with Mark Godfrey and receiving another, "I see…" Peter stared at Father Andrew, and asked, "What do you see, Father Andrew?"

"You don't understand, Peter…"

"Tell me, and I will understand, Father Andrew."

"There is a complex system of checks and balances that require many levels of input from approved personnel." Peter's cramped face of cynicism, encouraged Father Andrew to clarify the matter, with a simple, "It's a private process, where accusations of any nature are dealt with on an internal basis by the Archdiocese, and only the Archdiocese."

Peter was only eighteen but seemed much older when he looked at Father Andrew and said, "That is not right. It must be changed."

Father Andrew turned around in his small isolated church to make a point, and asked, "Why do think they sent me here?" As they walked out through the vestibule, Father Andrew stopped and said, "Listen to me Peter, it's not that I'm not hearing you. I believe every word that you say…but…unless you're one hundred percent sure, and you have concrete proof with witnesses that can speak with a loud voice, you cannot take down anyone in the clergy." Father Andrew placed his hand on Peter's back, and they continued down over the steps where they stopped at the base of Virgin Mary. The good priest looked up at her open arms, blessed himself and said, "Be vigilant, but be smart my son…Remember, as you continue your path towards the priesthood, you will find there is an unspoken law within the walls of the church." With a single finger placed over his lips, he whispered, "Secrecy." He removed his finger and continued, "Maybe…you can be the catalyst for change my son." There was a long silence with both trying to wrap their heads around the intensity of the conversation, then finally Father Andrew broke the silence, when he softly said, "You told me you're looking for a sign, Peter…Did you find it?"

Peter took a few steps, turned around, and replied, "No…but maybe this conversation is my sign."

From that time on, Peter continued to tread in the waters of his conflicted mind. Even though he continued to visit Father Andrew Truman on a weekly basis, the conversations never plateaued to the same feverish pitch, as the day his eyes were opened at the feet of the Virgin Mary.

Sundays came and went without any further hard-toned topics or cross words that could place wedges between Peter and Father Andrew. Seven years later, their friendship had been galvanized in absolute faith, without any further controversial considerations of the church, and its direction. In this lull of self-reckoning, Peter did not lose hope that his sign would appear from somewhere. At every opportunity and without exception, Mary Malone also ensured the pressure would remain, until the time he decided to accept his calling. Unbeknownst to everyone, the call they were waiting for, didn't appear from up above. Peter received his call, one dark night from the shining lights of another fallen angel.

Late one night, Peter went out for a walk in the light rain, to figure out the next step towards his holy path. At twenty-five years old, he was finally eligible to enter the seminary school in Ireland. If he decided to embark on the spiritual journey, it could be completed after five years of theology and practice. At the end of the five years, Peter would achieve his dream of becoming a full-fledge ordained priest. That night, when the rain came and went, Peter was still looking for the last sign that would push him over the top with a full commitment.

The light mist descending from the sky helped to cool his thoughts and clear his mind, as he walked along the dark road. At that moment in time, between the dense overhanging trees and the desire to make a decision, everything seemed to be closing in him.

The light rain that trickled down his face couldn't mask his disappointed feeling of not receiving a sign from above. Without some sort of divine intervention, Peter believed the invitation was lost by the unworthiness of his life. As he walked along with his final decision almost confirmed by the dampening rain, an oncoming car violently swerved and broke his span of attention.

Deep in thought and beyond the point of no return, there was no avoiding the inevitable collision course he was about to face. Peter had become transfixed in the moment and frozen in time, as the vehicle lights shone straight into his blinding eyes. With only one opportunity of movement, Peter closed his eyes and placed his life into the hands of God.

At full throttle, with the roar of the mighty v-eight engine and the heavy foot of a desperate driver, the end was coming fast. It was a seemingly suicide mission, as the speeding car lurched and swerved towards the closed eyed Peter Malone. Then, at the very last second, it turned right at the feet of Peter, flipped into the dense woods and finally lay steaming, under the slippery rain. Somehow, it had miraculously missed the praying pedestrian by the quick hand of its mad driver.

The wind from the flying projectile had pushed Peter's eyes wide open, where he looked down upon a crumpled car he had known extremely well. The remains of Kevin Callum's car were as far as the eyes could see under the streetlight and in the streaming rain. In the simmering smoke and buckling metal, Peter went up to his waist into the wet wooded area, where he found the bulk of the car. Somewhere in the midst of the mess, he knew, his friend needed him.

"KEVIN…KEVIN…CAN YOU HEAR ME?"

The screeching commotion had demanded the attention of the houses that watched over that sleepy road. In short, there were many others roaming through the blackness of the night and the darkness of the nearby trees, looking for wild-eyed Kevin Callum. It was a small community where everyone knew everything, good and bad, about everybody. Kevin had been a sweet young altar boy at one time, but since those unanswered days, he had gone down into a deep hole of delusion and despair.

In a deep hole of the wet mud, Gus Malone found Kevin alive with a silent smile on his broken face. Gus shouted at the top of his lungs, "I FOUND HIM! HE'S STILL

BREATHING!" While the responders quickly made their way over, Gus Malone realized the young man was bleeding profusely from every opening of his busted body. He leaned down at Kevin, and said softly, "You'll be okay, we'll call Father McKnight." The gushing blood from the gaping wound did not affect him like the sound of Father McKnight's name. With false strength and dying determination, young Kevin's soft smile quickly vanished with the pouring rain. He grabbed onto Gus, and with a raspy voice, he commanded, "Don't you bring that evil bastard here…"

Peter pushed his way through the bushes and busted trees until he stood with the rest of the onlookers. Gus signaled Peter to come to his side while he held onto young Kevin Callum's bloodied hand. Kneeling by the side of Kevin, Peter said, "You'll be okay Kev…"

"Is that you Peter?"

"Yes Kev, I'm here right by your side."

Gus looked at Peter, shook his head and said, "He doesn't want Father McKnight here…" He placed his hand on his son's shoulder and asked, "Will you say a prayer over him, son?"

Gus Malone knew Peter was the closest anyone could be to a real priest. He had watched him and Mary Malone recite every prayer known to man, with conviction and dedication. Peter took his neck chain with the small golden crucifix, made the sign of the cross, and said, "Father forgive him of his sins…He knew not, what he was doing…" In the middle of Peter's makeshift blessing, young Kevin cried out in vain, "It was him!"

"Who, Kevin?"

With last burst of existence, Kevin cried out, "He is the one…" Blood trickled down his still silent face, seeming to signal, the end had come for one tormented young man. Surrounded by the twisted car and emotional carnage, they had mistakenly believed, Kevin had spoken his final words. While the air-piercing sound of the ambulance siren wailed over the crowd, Kevin Callum's final breath and last words were wasted into the wind. Gus Malone and his praying son, did not hear Kevin finish, "It was him…*Father Sable abused me…*"

In the confusion of the Kevin's last brief words and the tragic moments of his final time on earth, the misinterpreted message opened up new possibilities. Peter's wishful thinking, had Kevin's last words engraved in his mind with, "It is him…He is the one." Peter Malone's faith had been signed and sealed, by the misunderstood message of God, from the dying lips of young Kevin Callum. His sign had been delivered loud and clear by a damaged altar boy and received by the desperate ears of Peter Malone.

Kevin Callum's tormented life had come to a tragic end, with a suicide ride that ended at the feet of Peter Malone. The emotional misery he suffered in the hands of Father Sable had come to a sad conclusion in the arms of his friend Peter Malone. In the murky mud of that dark night, the young man's life had finally ended under the suspicion of suicide and the misread message that he left behind.

For Peter Malone, the message was loud and clear, leaving no doubt in his mind. Preoccupied with his own flight to priestly stardom, Peter did not connect the dots with their childhood conversation, after the Mill Road incident and with Kevin's troubled life. He did not see the message of Kevin's last words, or the words he tried to tell when both young boys were at the playground so many years ago. Peter had been blinded by his own path that had been purposely planted by his mother, Mary Malone. Now, with the mistaken sign that he had been waiting for, Peter would enroll at the seminary college and prepare for his righteous path.

At the request of Kevin, from the note he had left behind, Father Andrew Truman would perform his funeral service at their parish. On that sad day, Father McKnight was not present at the somber service, when they finally lowered troubled Kevin Callum down into the cool ground. McKnight had conveniently left the parish to attend Archdiocese matters with his friends, Father Sable and Father Blake. In the absence of the three unwanted priests, Father Andrew Truman finished the funeral service with great sadness, while reflecting on conversation he had with Peter seven years prior. He stood in solitude and internalized the possibility of a connection with their conversation seven years ago. Considering the suspicious innuendos and whispering overtones that had reared from the silent walls of the Archdiocese, maybe it all had a connection with Kevin's young demise. Father Andrew shuddered to think about his silent response, when Peter spoke of Mark Godfrey's camping trip years ago. Lost in a turbulence of thought, Father Andrew was pleasantly surprised when Peter tapped him on the back and stopped him from drowning in his sea of regrets.

After the casket was laid to rest, Father Andrew and Peter Malone walked through the graveyard and began to talk. Surprisingly to Father Andrew, Peter did not start the conversation in the direction he had expected. On that day, suspicion, doubt and denial remained with the fallen ones that surrounded them. Among the dead souls, Peter exuberantly expressed his decision. "Father Andrew I received my sign…"

"Sign of what, Peter?"

"A sign to enter the priesthood." Puzzled, Father Andrew looked about gravestones and asked, "Where did the sign come from?"

"It was delivered by Kevin Callum, on the night he died…"

"Kevin Callum?"

"Yes, on the night he died," he said, "*It is him…He is the one…*"

"Wow, Peter…I don't know what to say…"

"The bible says, the lord works in mysterious ways. I guess he used Kevin, to show me the way."

There was a long silence, where both were trying to comprehend the magnitude of the misunderstanding. Peter knew by the look on Father Andrew's face, he wasn't fully accepting his story at face value. Father Andrew understood by the look on Peter's face, he believed his own far-fetched story without question. Both were at an impasse as they stood by the stone-faced statues that stared down without judgment. Peter looked upon the high gravestone in front of him and broke the silence, "That person must have had great prominence." Father Andrew turned his back on the big gravestone, looked down upon the lowly grave with the wooden cross, and said, "I buried both…but the person in this grave…had the biggest heart and purest soul."

The cool wind blew up the graveyard path, giving both men the signal to begin their walk down the hill. As they walked, Father Andrew Truman said, "If you truly believe, that you have received a sign, then who am I to judge this great apparition."

Peter watched Father Andrew intently, as he continued, "I know…I believe in you, as a person and that's all that matters to me." Father Andrew stopped at the gate of the graveyard, made the sign of the cross on Peter's forehead, and said, "Go with God."

Later in the day, Peter informed his parents of his final decision to embark on the journey to the seminary school in Ireland. Gus's blank face did not show a hint of surprise or a spark of excitement. For he knew full well that this day had been planned by his wife from the first time she laid her eyes upon the seventh son of a seventh son. Mary Malone, on the other hand, could not control her display of emotion. Her dream had come into fruition with her golden child materializing into a man of the cloth. Molded from the dust of Mary Malone's miraculous vision, her son Peter was cast on the path to salvation. In the limelight of his mother's adoration and the lukewarm blessing of his father, Peter realized he had one call to make before his revealing day was over.

"Hello Brother. How are you?"

"Been worse, Peter…"

"Damian, I got some news for you."

"I have news for you too, Peter."

"I'm heading for Ireland, to the seminary college."

"Well, I'm happy for you Peter, but be careful over there…"

"What can happen to me there?"

"Be careful, that's all Peter…Just be careful…"

"Thanks Damian, I'll be okay. What's your news?"

"Peter, do you remember Mark Godfrey?"

"Yes…he was an altar boy with us."

"Well…He's a bum, on the streets here in the city…and I talk to him all the time."

"That's sad Damian…so sad…"

"He's wasted and blabbering gibberish every time I see him Peter."

"What a pity…He was a good kid back then."

"Peter do remember the camping incident, you told me about?"

"Yes, but he would never talk about it."

"Well, Peter, he continually mumbles about priests and camping…"

"Tell him I'll pray for him in Ireland, Damian…"

"Right on."

"Take care of yourself, Damian."

"Keep your back to the wall over in that college, Peter."

Keep your back to the wall, wasn't something Peter considered, when he envisioned living at the seminary college. He didn't know why his brother would say such strange things about a college that possessed only priestly goals. For a moment, Peter wondered if the city had twisted Damian's overactive imagination. Realizing that there was too much to miss with his back to the wall, Peter refocused his attention on the luck of the Irish. Just maybe, with help from the power of the church, he could help the lost soul of Mark Godfrey when he returned as an ordained priest.

Two months later, Peter and his parents were at the international airport ready for the flight to Ireland. When Mary Malone had finished her long emotional goodbyes, Gus took Peter to side and said, "Remember son, no matter what happens in the future, be true to yourself."

"Thanks Pop, by I believe I'm doing the right thing for myself."

"Well, that's good son…I'm just giving you an option, that's all."

"I appreciate that Pop."

With the announcement of the final gate, Gus shook his son's hand and left him with, "Sometimes, a guy can be in the right church…but the wrong pew…"

"Goodbye Pop."

Chapter 8

Green Grass and Dark Discoveries

The green grass of Ireland looked lush and inviting, as Peter's plane began to descend toward the Dublin International Airport. He had dreamt of the time he would set foot on Irish soil, but as the plane decelerated, nothing prepared him for how exhilarated he really felt the moment before touchdown. Wheels down and ready to hit the cobble stones, Peter Malone was rearing to receive Dublin, Ireland with all his heart and soul.

At the baggage carousel, Peter eyed a man holding a sign with his name printed below the banner of St. Brennan's College. He walked over and politely asked, "Are you driving me to the college?" In a strong Irish brogue, the man with the crooked sign said, "Well I'm not er' to pick me nose lad."

"Okay…I'll be right with you. There's one more bag left on the carousel."

"What are ya do'n with all da baggage? Yer go'n to be a Priest not a Pope."

"Well sir…I wanted to be sure I had sufficient clothes."

"Then, go get yer shite, and we'll get da fook out of here."

The driver was wee bit crustier than he expected, but Peter was not completely thrown off by the sound of bluntness. He actually took comfort in the Irishman's crude approach and his blunt honesty. It made him think of home and his brother's straight shooting, no nonsense attitude. Lost in a daze of thinking about downhome, Peter was startled when the driver grabbed the bag from his hand, and said, "Yer like an old nun…Let's get go'n b'y…"

At full speed and damn the consequences, there was no holding back from that point on. The seminary college was located south of the Dublin International Airport, in the county of Kildare and in town of Kilbride. Far from the hustle and bustle of the busy city of Dublin, Kilbride was nestled by the River Rye, a major tributary of the great River Liffey. Peter had never seen anything like the narrow roads and the steep rock walls. It appeared to him, like the close towering walls seemed to squeeze them into submission, as they squeaked through at high speed. With his white-knuckled grip on the edge of his seat, he suggested, "We don't have to hurry, there's plenty of time Mr…"

"Call me Paddy."

"Well Mr. Paddy, I'm day ahead of the schedule, so we can take our time…If you don't mind…"

"Lasts name is Ryan, and don't go get'n yer white collar too stiff. Old Paddy will get you to Benny's in one piece."

Ten uncomfortable minutes later, Paddy finally slowed down and turned up a long driveway with the sign St. Brennan's College proudly posted out in front. A pleasant looking, round faced priest, stepped up to the car and waited until Peter stepped out upon the old cobbled stone.

"Mr. Malone, it's nice to meet you at last. I'm Father Kelly." With a hardy handshake and friendly greeting, the round-faced priest turned to the driver and said, "Paddy, you'll have to go back to the airport. Another student has arrived much earlier than expected…and Paddy can you take Mr. Malone's bags to his room."

There was no mistaking Paddy's displeasure with his dynamic list of things to do. While Father Kelly turned his back, Paddy leaned into Peter and whispered with a crusty tone, "Do I look like a fook'n bag man to you?" Peter silently grinned, as he watched the grumpy gentleman shuffle off with his two heavy bags.

Father Kelly signaled Peter to follow and as he walked, he said, "At St. Brennan's we believe the student comes first…"

"I'm really looking forward to the theology courses."

"I applaud your enthusiasm but…first, we must walk, before we run my son."

The afternoon came with an avalanche of introductions to the various college instructors, staff and priests. Everyone was cordial, as they welcomed Peter into their celibate world of white washed walls adorned with dark framed pictures of priests from the past. After the major introductions, and brief walk through the old establishment, Peter was shown to his room at the end of a long hall. Father Kelly knocked on the door, opened it and said, "These are you roommates, Mr. Thomas Barker and Mr. Stephan Easton. I will expect you promptly in one hour at the dining hall." The door shut with an echo and Father Kelly left Peter overwhelmed and in the care of his two new roommates.

Thomas Barker was quick to reach out his hand, "Call me Tom."

"Nice to meet you, Tom."

"And…this is his Eminence Pope Stephan…" The fictious greeting broke the ice between the two men with a hard laugh that didn't extend beyond their corner of the room. Standing at the ironing board with a stiff shirt in his hand, Mr. Easton sent them a frosty stare, and said, "I don't find disrespecting the Pope humorous, Mr. Thomas…"

Mr. Stephen Easton turned his attention to the new student and respectfully said, "It is indeed nice to you meet you. Maybe we can study theology together."

Thomas clapped his hands loudly, and interjected, "Lighten up Steve…we're all friends here. Aren't we, Pope Peter?"

Precisely at six, the dining bell rang, and the resident students came filing out of their rooms for their formal evening meal. At the dining table, Thomas nudged Peter with his elbow, and said, "It's a bit stiff around here, but you'll get used to it." Before Peter could respond, another bell rang out, and then Father Kelly blessed everything from the food, to the farmer in the field, before one bite was devoured by the devout droolers.

On the way out of the dining hall, Father Kelly tapped Peter on the arm and said, "Come with me." Further up the hall, away from the hustle and bustle of the clearing students, Father Kelly stopped, pointed towards a door at the end of the hall, and said, "That's a small room dedicated for student phone calls. You have a call from your Brother."

"Hello Damian."

"Hello Peter…"

"Is everything okay? I'm only here one day and you're calling."

"Do you remember our conversation about Mark Godfrey?"

"Yes…"

"Do you remember I told you he was living on the streets?"

"Yes…"

"Peter…poor Mark died of an overdose…"

"Noooo…"

There was a minute, where both men could only swallow their emotions, as they pictured young Mark, back when they were innocent boys. They were lost in time, under trees of the beautiful church garden that Father McKnight had callously cut to the core. Peter softly said, "Everything changed after the incident on Mill Road…"

"I know Peter…I know all about it…"

"But Mark would not speak to anyone. How do you know what happened?"

"One night…I found him on the streets and offered him a room in my apartment."

"Did he accept, Damian?"

"No…He didn't go there, but he went somewhere else." There was a short silence, then Damian took a long breath, and said, "I stayed with him on the street that cold night…I just couldn't leave him there by himself. Late into the night, when we were both numb with coldness, I fell asleep and he fell into deep depression. I awoke later, to find him with a dirty syringe hanging from his arm and a blank look upon his face. With his last words and his last breath, he told me, that Father Blake abused him…"

Hanging on to every word, with deep regret that he didn't do enough to help the boy, Peter said, "Our suspicions were right…"

With a short pause, Damian quickly added, "Mark didn't go into details." Damian's voice began to break, as he continued, "But if you saw his sunken eyes…you would know. The details were written upon his broken face."

Salty tears could be tasted from sea to sea, on the night that truth had been delivered by one brother who heard the truth, and another who had seen the light. Damian pulled himself together and mustered up the courage to say, "I'm not saying all your priest friends are like those three priestly pricks in our parish…I'm just calling…to warn you…Keep your eyes open Brother…"

On a day that seemed to never end, Peter laid his head on a foreign pillow and listened to the echoes of his mind. With his losing the battle of sleep and the continual tossing and turning, Thomas Barker's voice came from darkness of the night.

"Don't worry, Peter…It's a lot to take in, but it will work out." From the other side of the room, Peter replied, "You don't understand Tom, there is plenty at work, that you can't see." With a roll of the bed springs, Thomas responded, "Trust me, I understand that there's more to our society than most would ever know, but that doesn't mean we have to give up on something that we all believe in." In the corner of the room, with random sounds of seminary students coming and going down the hall, Peter pondered over Thomas Barker's ability to fathom the depth of darkness that existed in his home parish. He lay on the bed in the stillness of night, while the voice of Mr. Stephan Easton broke the stuttering silence with a simplistic statement, "Just believe in yourself and God…and the rest will work out…"

The week went by in total torment for Peter, as he settled into seminary studies. Hard as he tried, Peter couldn't stop thinking about the abusive carnage that resulted in Mark Godfrey's death. Unaware, that Father Blake was only the tip of the iceberg, the remaining two priests, Father Sable and Father McKnight lay silently submerged from his suspicion. In his mind, Peter knew something must be done to stop the one demented priest, who had deviated from the righteous path of priesthood. On the following Sunday night, Peter picked up the phone and placed a call to the only person who had a priestly rank and would never back down from the truth.

Peter remembered the day, back in Father Andrew's parish, when he told him of his suspicions about Father Blake. At the foot of the Virgin Mary, Father Andrew Truman's reluctant response was based on the need to be one hundred percent sure and with witnesses that would speak loudly. With Damian's true words from the mouth of dying Mark Godfrey, he believed he was one hundred percent sure that he was making a good call to the right person.

"Hello Father Andrew…"

"Peter! What a surprise! How are you doing over there?"

"I'm doing well with the seminary studies, but not so well, with my faith in my fellow man…"

"What's wrong, Peter?"

"Do you remember, years ago when we spoke of Mark Godfrey…and you told me to be one hundred percent sure, with a witness that would speak loudly?"

"Yes…I do…"

Peter went on to tell Damian's tragic story of Mark Godfrey's final demise on the streets of the city. He described the pain the poor young man had endured while cold and hungry, searching for the innocence that he lost on Mill Road years before. Drug-induced and burdened by the past abuse at the hands of the preying priest, he explained how Mark finally took his life in the arms of his brother, Damian Malone.

Father Andrew measured every word and when Peter had finished briefing him on the incident, he began to dig deeper for details. "Peter please don't take this the wrong way, the depth of my question is only because I care…" Peter cleared his throat and replied, "I understand, the case has to be rock solid to proceed."

"That's correct Peter because if there is one loophole, it will not succeed."

"What is the question?"

"When Mark died in the arms of Damian, did he give any specifics on what happened?"

"He didn't come out and say everything Father Andrew. It must have been too painful for him to express."

Father Andrew became too silent for too long. Peter continued, "The message was crystal clear by the expression on his face and the fact that he said with his own lips…Father Blake abused me…"

"I'm sorry Peter, but this Archdiocese has deep pockets and is more powerful than you will ever realize. It has powerful lawyers that will rip the account of those scanty details into shreds…"

"Like Father Blake ripped Mark Godfreys life in shreds, Father Andrew."

"Yes…just like that…"

"But…Father Andrew…There is no doubt, in Damian's mind and my heart, that Father Blake abused a young Mark Godfrey."

"And there is no doubt in my mind and my heart, as well…I am with you, not against you."

Peter's frustration could be felt over the phone, pushing Father Andrew to say, "In the face of what I know will happen, I will take this to the highest level."

"Really Father Andrew?"

"Yes, Peter…I will not let you down, at any cost."

"God bless you, Father Andrew."

"God bless us all, Peter."

In the good hands of Father Andrew, Peter was given hope that some sort of justice would prevail, and Father Blake would be removed from the priesthood. Even though Father Andrew knew his own faith was sealed, he would place it all on the line for truth and the ones he believed in. That night, sleep came easy for Peter knowing a sacrificial angel was watching over their cause. Back in home parish, sleep never came that night. Father Andrew Truman fully understood, no mortal or angel, could crack the back of an establishment that had no intention of restoring anyone's faith.

As time went on at the seminary college, Peter excelled in his academic and theology grades. Knowing the pressure of attaining and maintaining good grades came with a substantial psychological cost to the students, the college curriculum allowed for relaxation outings throughout the program. As the schedule moved on, one of these outings finally came up on their daily planner. On the following Monday, they would be off by bus, to Blarney Castle, over to Dingle and back home to St. Brennan's College. It was going to include the full Irish experience, aboard the college bus, driven by the colorful Paddy Ryan.

At seven sharp on Monday morning, all the seminary students had boarded the bus and were ready for relaxation. Knowing that old Paddy had a hairpin trigger, Thomas Barker shouted, "What's the holdup…We'll never get back to Kilbride in time, at this rate." Paddy shut the door and put the bus in first gear causing Stephen Easton to exclaim, "You can't go without Father Kelly!" Paddy took the bus out of gear, quickly opened the door and said, "Make up yer fook'n minds."

Father Kelly appeared from the corner of the building and boarded the bus without any further comments from the impatient Paddy Ryan. He entered the bus and said, "Sorry for the delay but I heard on the radio, there is a major security breach at a Maze prison up in County Antrim." Paddy closed the door and Father Kelly continued, "Thirty-eight escaped and now they're running for their lives…" He blessed himself, and said, "Let's say a pray for their safety before we go."

Paddy revved up the engine after receiving a nod from Father Kelly, and then they were finally off to Blarney

Castle for a quick kiss upon the rough lips of the famous blarney stone. Breezing through the towns and squeezing by villages, Peter noted to Thomas, "Paddy don't slow down for anything…"

"Nope, not even for old nuns."

"Makes for an interesting time, Tom!"

"I'm sure we're in for a wild ride, Peter."

It was a Monday, which meant the Blarney castle parking lot was bare and the opportunity to explore seemed endless. Without the weekend crowds, Paddy drove right up the entrance gate, opened the bus door and said, "Mind yer step lads…" Thomas was the last in line to leave the bus, but couldn't help himself, when he got to the side of Paddy and sarcastically suggested, "Paddy you better not go too far, Father Kelly won't be happy if you're late." Paddy did a swift head shift to the right and left and quickly replied, "I don't give flying fook what he thinks."

Looking up at the stone structure, Peter asked, "Where is the Blarney stone located?"

Stephen Easton had been there before and was quick to answer, "The pamphlet says it is right to the top and it's a tight squeeze all the way." Thomas quickly added, "Then, let's get going…" Noticing Stephen was not following, Peter stopped and asked, "Aren't you coming Stephen?"

"No."

"Why?"

"I don't believe in idol rocks, Peter."

"But…" Before Peter could continue queestioning Stephen, Thomas grabbed his arm and said, "Leave him where he wants to be…" Then he leaned in, and whispered, "He's weird, let's go."

On top of the Castle, the other students had finished kissing the famous Blarney Stone and now it was their turn. With a grab from the old attendant, they went upside down and inside out, until they stared at a shiny stone that the whole world had kissed. Taking too long, the old attendant said, "Come on lad, I haven't got all day." In one second, the kiss was sealed and then they were swung back to the landing, where the attendant pointed two fingers towards his coin bucket.

Back down on the ground, Peter found Stephen alone in the castle garden with his rosary beads in his hands. He went up to him, and said, "That was a lot to do about nothing…" Stephen shrugged his shoulders, "It's not everyone's cup of tea."

The big yellow bus promptly hauled up in front of the castle at the precise time and Paddy Ryan laid heavy upon the blaring horn. There was plenty of ground to cover and he knew there would be no wasted time, as long as the horn worked well. Once again, Father Kelly was the last on board and once again, he had another news update from up north. "Well lads, I just heard news report…The escapees from Maze prison have been all caught." Paddy struck the wheel, and cried out, "Fook'n bastards!"

Father Kelly sharply replied, "Now, Paddy…we'll have no more of that today." He bowed his head and said, "We'll have a short prayer for the b'ys who have been injured, on this terrible day."

The bus pulled out shortly after the prayer and accelerated towards Dingle with a heavy heart. In a land where the green grass and foggy weather mingled in complete harmony, life for so many was difficult, dealing with troubles of humanity. The day quickly flew by, as they traveled from village to town on the narrow roads at full throttle. With a quick meal of fresh fish in Dingle, they headed back on a straight path to Dublin, feeling refreshed and ready for the seclusive walls of St. Brennan's College.

It was late when they got back to the College and everyone was tired except Peter Malone. He knew the timing would be perfect to speak in the phone room, without others waiting in line. In his mind, he felt the time had come, when long awaited questions could be answered by his friend Father Andrew. Peter picked up the phone and dialed a long-distance number that was going to be a quick call and a long distant memory.

An old lady answered with a shaky, "Hello…"

"Hello Ma'am. Could I speak to Father Truman, please?"

The old woman replied, "Father Andrew Truman is no longer the parish priest here. But if you would like to speak to Father Blake, I can get him for you."

"No ma'am, that won't be necessary."

The absence of Father Andrew and the presence of Father Blake spoke louder than words could say. Peter finally understood why his friend had been hesitant to fight the devoted sanctuary of silence. The apparent action from the Archdiocese left no doubt in his mind, they would not be tolerating inquiries from outlying priests. Once again, Father Andrew Truman had been on the front lines and found himself a casualty in the line of duty for the truth. In a time when dissent by disillusioned priests were dealt with a heavy hand, Father Truman was not afraid to speak out. Now, with Father Truman missing in the action for spreading the word of truth, Peter was left alone to fight a silent battle, from the beautiful green fields of Ireland.

Chapter 9

Conversations of Clarity

The attempts to contact Father Andrew were in vain, as the weeks carried on and the courses continued without hearing from his friend. Time and time again, Peter would call the Archdiocese requesting Father Truman's whereabouts, and in return, he would receive vague responses accompanied by undefined answers. Some suggested, he was on sabbatical in the Middle East and others implied, he had taken a break in an undisclosed location. The run-around of ambiguous answers had Peter going in circles until one evening he stumbled on a snippet of information from his unsuspecting mother.

On his monthly call home to his family, the conversations were mainly generic without controversial topics that would cause unnecessary tensions. Peter knew his mother's unwavering devotion to Father McKnight would not falter, unless the truth came out and the dark secrets were revealed. Knowing she was a close ally and would have been privy with Father Truman's situation, Peter approached his missing priest dilemma from a different angle, using reverse psychology.

"Yes Mom, all is going well here at the College…"

"Do you need anything, Peter?"

"No…but could you ask Father Andrew to send me the book he spoke about yesterday?"

"Ahh…you…spoke to Father Andrew?"

"Just for a minute…"

"But I thought there was no communications up in the Northern Territories…"

With a quick change of subject, he smartly backed away from his white lie and onto the darker conversation about his brother Damian. Peter was fully aware that any discussion about the wayward son, would send his mother's blood pressure up and block any previous temporary thoughts. Introducing Damian as a decoy, wasn't something he was proud of, but with the high stakes of having Father Blake in the company of children, he was willing to throw his understanding brother under his mother's bus. The price was worth the cost, to squeeze out that slip of the tongue by his unaware mother. Elements of extreme weather were now his focus because he knew they had placed Father Andrew Truman, far where the sun didn't shine, and the cold wind kept his mouth shut tight.

The Northern Territories may have been isolated from the Archdiocese, but Peter had close connections that could help close the long-distance gap. Just before he ended the call with his mother, Peter requested to speak with his father. Peter was aware that his father was not a fan of the phone but under the circumstances of knowing Gus's past connection with the North, he waited patiently while Mary Malone coxed his father reluctantly to the phone.

"Peter?"

"Hello Pop."

"What's so important?"

"Is Mom close by?"

"No."

"Good…I need your help…"

Over the years Gus had been aware of the suspicious behavior of the Father McKnight and his two friends. He also knew that Father Truman was missing in action at his previous parish. It did not take him long to quickly connected the dots and come up to speed with Peter's disclosure on his mother's loose lips.

"Peter, I wasn't aware they sent him up North."

"I know…but I need to speak with him now Pop."

"There is a way…as you know, I worked up there years ago."

"I know, Pop."

"Leave it with me. I'll make some calls."

Later, back in the room, Peter lay on the bed with his hands over his face. Stephen was out and Thomas was left in the room, to watch his friend wallow in anguish. Thomas Barker was not the type of person to leave well enough alone, when things were obviously wrong. Thomas went over and sat by the side of Peter's bed and asked, "What's up, Pete?"

"It's all good, Tom."

"Is that so…well, you don't look very good with that long face."

"You don't understand…"

"Oh, I understand more than you know, Peter."

"Tom, we are from two different countries."

"It's all the same my friend. No matter where you're from."

"I don't know, Tom…"

"Well, tell me and then I'll know."

The topic was a sore spot in Peter's life, where the ugly wounds caused by outcast priests had crossed the line of decency within their vulnerable parish. He was ashamed, to put forth the possibility that dark atrocities had occurred in the safety of his hometown. He was embarrassed there was nothing he could say that would erase the past, without affecting the future. Peter Malone was concerned that he may even affect the trajectory of his colleagues' path, with the release of such negative news about their religious establishment. In spite of it all, Thomas's sincere request to help caused him to finally put his guard down, and say, "I don't want to influence your path to priesthood, Tom."

"If my path is that fragile, I'm in deep trouble. Let's have it…What's on your mind, Peter?"

"There are dark forces within our own walls my friend."

"If you're going to tell me something, please don't say it in riddles, Peter."

Peter quickly realized that Thomas needed the straight facts with clarity and with that in mind, he began to explain, "Back in our parish there were despicable acts done on innocent kids right under the watch of everyone…Three priests have gone against what we believe in. One of those, I know, has committed egregious acts on a friend who later overdosed in tragic grief." Thomas nodded his head slowly and said, "I'm not completely shocked my friend. These things have happened before and will happen again."

"Well, Tom, I was hoping it wouldn't happen again…"

"What do that mean, Peter?"

"My very good friend Father Andrew was in the process of addressing the Archdiocese about the incident."

"Did he succeed, Peter?"

Peter sat up straight and replied, "I haven't heard anything since he committed to address the abuse."

"Sounds like he's silenced, Peter…"

There was a long silence between the young men, until Thomas simply said, "It's all a game, Peter. A game where if you don't play by their rules, you'll find yourself without a pew."

"I don't believe that, Tom…not for one minute…"

"Well…I do…I was also abused when I was a kid."

Words could not stop the sinking feeling, Peter felt with Thomas's heavy words of abuse.

"I'm sorry, Tom."

"It was a long time ago…"

"Was it the parish priest?"

"No…no…not the clergy…It was a friend of the family."

"I'm deeply sorry, Tom."

"Well…I got over it…I buried it deep within, and never brought it up again."

Peter looked at his friend and replied, "Until now…"

"Yes…until now…"

"The point is Peter, some men are going to do despicable acts, no matter what station they have in life. It's a game, Peter…a game…"

Peter placed his head down and sadly left his friend with a solemn, "God didn't play games on the cross, Tom."

"I know that, Peter…I'm just saying…don't put your trust in men…"

The following Sunday Peter was called out from class by Father Kelly. He didn't look pleased, when he warned, "We will not tolerate calls during class hours but for this one time, since it is your father, we will allow it." Father Kelly bluntly pointed towards the phone room and said, "Make it quick lad…"

"Hello son."

"Did you find him?"

"Yes, he's up in North West Territories in a community called Inuvik."

"Can I call him?"

"No, but he can call you from the power station. It's the only place in the community with a phone connection."

"When will he call, Pop?"

"Sunday at eight PM, Greenwich Mean time."

"At least, I'll finally get answers…"

"Son, the answer is loud and clear…"

"What do you mean, Pop?"

"He's up where the sun doesn't shine…He's in Inuvik."

Late that night, as he lay in his bed Thomas asked, "I heard you had a call today…" Peter wasn't asleep, he had been rolling in his bed at the far end of the room. He replied, "It was my Pop. He told me I would get a call from Father Andrew on Sunday."

"I hope it's good news, Peter."

"Yes…me too, Tom."

"Your friend Father Andrew sounds like a solid guy."

"He was dealt a rotten deal, from our Archdiocese…especially since they found out he is gay."

"Wow, that guy has courage, Pete…I wish I was as strong."

"What do you mean, Tom?"

"I'm gay too, Peter."

The week that would never end, finally came to a crashing conclusion with revelations from Thomas Barker. A deep confession from Thomas, in the support of Peter's troubling dilemma, introduced a new dimension of reality. In the time when the Catholic church looked down upon the evil acts of homosexuality, Peter's two friends were caught between something they could not control. It was a conundrum of complex ironic twists and turns, where those at the top, turned away from the truth and towards the protection of their own power. This ironic atmosphere had permeated the walls of the Archdiocese but not the ones who believed in sanctum of truth. Peter's eyes had been opened, by the honesty of his friends who spoke the truth, and by the dishonesty of those who spoke nothing but lies.

Early on Sunday, Peter spread the word of his anticipated call for later that evening. Frustration and bewilderment were not an uncommon site to see on some faces from time to time within the walls of St. Brennan's College. Every now and again, a student would submerge into the silent depth of their mind, under the magnitude of their religious undertaking. Those difficult days were often impressed upon a sad face, which indicated a wide berth was needed. With Peter's long-standing face in the classroom, the other students stood down and gave Peter plenty of opportunity to take his awaited call.

At eight o'clock, the bell chime came with a sinking feeling for the anxious Peter Malone. Maybe a snow squall had taken the line down, or maybe the Archdiocese had given the order of no communication for Father Andrew Truman. As time went by, without the ringing tone, the free flow of possibilities and reasons seemed to suggest, the call would never be made. At twelve o'clock, Peter had given up hope, until Father Kelly knocked, poked his head in the doorway, and said, "Someone's on the line. They're waiting for you Peter."

Peter raced down the hallway and with a breathless gasp, he said, "Hello…"

"Hello, Peter…"

"You're a site for sore eyes, Father Andrew…"

"It's good to hear your voice too, Peter."

"Seems like they really wanted you out of range."

"I guess they wanted to freeze me out up here."

"Is it really cold there, Father Andrew?"

"Not as cold, as the wind that blows behind the Archdiocese walls."

"What happened when you brought up Mark Godfrey's abuse, by Father Blake?"

"Let's just say, the conversation became very frosty Peter. Every time I introduced a point, I was shot down by Bishop Stone. He was not open to any discussion at all. In fact, the more I tried to tell him what happened, the more he became agitated."

Peter's frustration grew with every revelation of blatant disregard for justice. Realizing he was on limited phone time, Peter asked, "What about taking it to the police?"

There was a long breath from Father Andrew, then he said, "You're still not getting it Peter…"

"Getting what?"

"There is no fighting the Archdiocese. You may as well forget it…"

"But…Father Andrew…surely they can't let Father Blake be in the company of young boys again."

"Peter…Father Blake has been assigned to my former parish."

The devastating news silenced Peter for a second, and then he said, "And…your life as a priest is ruined for nothing…"

"Peter…Listen to me. They can put me on the moon…I don't care anymore…I'm ordained a priest and I will die a priest who believes. Even though they don't believe in what or who I am, I know God believes in me and that's all that matters."

"But Father Andrew…where do we go from here?"

"According to the wall of snow I'm facing, it's up to you, to change the direction of our Archdiocese."

"I'm not even a priest yet…"

"You have just over two years to go, and then you will be needed here more than ever."

"To take on Father Blake?"

Father Andrew didn't know the full details of the other two priests, but he had heard many rumors and felt it was time to put it all on the table for Peter. With great reluctance to place the heavy burden upon the young shoulders of his friend, Father Andrew took a breath and said, "The damage to our faith may be deeper than you know, Peter."

"How deep, Father Andrew?"

"There are rumors and innuendos pointing in the direction of Father Sable and Father McKnight."

"I never liked those priests, but I could never imagine they would go to the depths that Father Blake did…"

"I believe Bishop Stone it's the only one who can fathom the extent of their demented reach."

"If Bishop Stone is privy to this information, where can anyone go with this, Father Andrew?"

"Monsignor Murphy is your only chance. He may have faults, like us all, but he is a holy man that can be reached."

"I…don't know Father Andrew…I don't know if I have the strength for this…"

"Peter…listen to me…whatever you decide, do it for yourself."

"I remember, a long time ago…you told me to follow my true path."

Father Andrew's time was up with a tap of the shoulder from the power plant manager. He left Peter with the last sincere words, "Only you will know what truth is…only you…"

Another sleepless night came and went with a continual barrage of questions that brought Peter to a crossroads of reckoning. Two and a half years had passed and two and a half years remaining, Peter had reached the halfway point at the seminary college. Overwhelmed with the task remaining and disillusioned by the treatment of Father Andrew, Peter went to the small college chapel to muster up the courage he needed to continue.

Peter lit up one of the candles and stood in front of the small altar. As he lifted his head to the ceiling, a mild voice said, "I love this chapel…it brings me peace." Peter turned sharply, regained his composure and said, "I didn't realize you were in here."

"Sorry for startling you."

"No worries…"

"You're usually never here alone. What brings you in here today, Peter?"

"Just looking for answers…"

"Can I help?"

In the dim lit chapel, Peter went over and sat down by Stephen on the small pew. Even though most of the students felt Stephen was almost too religiously fanatical, Peter believed he was the only one who was completely true to himself and his faith. He knew, if they were dedicated to the priesthood, they all should emulate his devotion and dedication. Peter looked at his friend and said, "Much has happened recently that has put doubt in my mind."

"Doubt in yourself, Peter?"

"Yes…I don't know if I can continue my spiritual journey."

Peter had expected his stringently religious friend to return with a rigid response, attached with various references from the bible, but he did not. Stephen laid his hand upon his shoulder and sincerely said, "It's okay to have doubt…everyone has doubt…It's a process we all go through in finding our true souls."

He did not want to tell his friend the complete details of his ongoing dilemma back in his parish, in fear it would affect his own personal perspective. The demented priests and the negative response from the Archdiocese would not be shared with his friend. Peter approached Stephen in a different way, when he asked vaguely, "What if there are some among us, who do not walk on the righteous path?"

He looked straight at Stephen and asked, "What if there is evil among us and we do nothing about it?"

Stephen replied, "You have troubles deeper than the ocean my friend…" Stephen paused, stared up at the front of the alter and said, "Sin has been with humanity since the beginning and will be with us till it's time…whether it is on the inside or on the outside of our walls. Evil is at work, everywhere and all the time. I don't know what to say about humanities battle with sin. All I know is…be true to yourself."

"But Stephen…what if a priest has committed the unspeakable?"

Stephen stood up, went to front of the church, returned and said, "Let's pray, Peter…for the victim and for the soul of that priest."

Peter walked out of the chapel feeling better than he had in many days. In the darkness of that the small chapel, he had found a glimmer of hope and new appreciation for his faithful friend. Under the light of the low burning candles, Peter's troubled conscience was relieved with aid of reflection and a new perspective. It all came just in time, when time off from the St. Brennan's College had been scheduled in.

At the half-way milestone, it was customary to be given an extended seminary sabbatical, where the students could reflect on their path to priesthood. The College administration understood very well that during this sabbatical the path would be lost for some and found for others. In the case of Peter and his seminary friends, this lost and found scenario played out exactly as expected, upon the streets of old Dublin.

Chapter 10

Sobering Sabbatical

It was the midway point into their program and time for the customary sabbatical for the seminary students. At this midway point in their program, the option of where to go and what to do was left at the discretion of the students. Normally, most would head home and spend time with family and friends while they reflected on their spiritual journey. In some cases, the students would remain on the grounds of St. Brennan's College and meditate in the solace of their chapel. For other students, the sabbatical provided a time to travel and ponder their futures without outside influence or the inside seduction of peace and tranquility. As the time came, for selecting which option to take, Peter and Thomas had a conversation that would take them both on separate paths.

"Are you heading home, Peter?"

"I'm not sure…"

"Well, they need an answer soon."

"There's plenty I need to consider…"

"Why don't you consider coming with me, Peter?"

"Where are you heading?"

"I'm staying in Dublin and renting a small apartment for the duration."

"I don't know…"

"There's two rooms and we can share expenses."

"I'll think about it, Tom."

Later that evening, Peter was in the middle of his customary call with his mother, when she began to reel out her intended schedule. Mary Malone had her plans in place, with every day full of flashing her own priest in front of everyone that she could find. As she spoke, her predetermined path for him flashed by in Peter's mind, causing him to stop and rethink his own direction. While Mary Malone continually poured out her good intentions, Peter interrupted the one-way conversation and stopped his mother in her consecrated tracks.

"Mom, you'll have to cancel any engagements you have made on my behalf."

"Why…what's wrong son?"

"There's nothing wrong. I will not be coming home during my sabbatical."

"Where are you going, Peter?"

"I'll be staying with a friend in Dublin."

"Has it been approved by the College?"

"Yes…I'll be fine…I'll be in the company of another seminary student."

"But…what about my plans?"

"They'll have to wait. I will be making my own plans from now on, Mom."

On the following week it was time to inform the College's administration, on where they would be taking their sabbatical. Thomas Barker was about to walk into the

Father Kelly's office, when Peter tapped him on the back, and asked, "Is that room still available?"

"We're going to have a great time, Peter."

"It may be the change of scenery I'm looking for."

"It won't hurt to get away from the prying eyes of these walls too…"

One week later Peter was packed and ready to go, except for one remaining task to do before they headed out for the college bus. He was told that Stephan had not requested external leave from the college and he also knew where he could find his spiritual friend. Just inside the chapel door, Peter found contented Stephen Easton alone and kneeling in front of a small altar. Stephen smiled, and said, "I see you're all ready to go."

"You should take a break from this place, Stephen."

"I am, where I want to be, Peter."

Peter smiled, tapped him on the back and said, "I envy you, my friend."

Stephen sat back on the pew and replied, "It really doesn't matter what you choose to do in life…as long as you know you are at peace inside."

"Is that how I will know?"

"Know what, Peter?"

"That priesthood is my path."

"Only you will know the answer to that question, my friend."

Stephen could hear Tom calling from a distance, signaling the bus had arrived to pick them up. He reached out his hand and said, "Maybe you will find clarity in the city."

Peter shook his hand and replied, "I'm open for answers."

From the hallway, Thomas shouted, "Come on Malone…Or Paddy's going to bust an artery…"

"Got to go, Stephen."

"Good luck, Peter!"

The bus pulled away with a fresh-faced seminary student pressed upon every dew filled window. In the early morning hours, as old Dublin city began to wake, the sights and sounds stirred a sense of new beginning within the young men. Passing by the Liffey, the mist hung softly above the river, as they made their way over the cobbled streets. In short, they came to O'Connell Street, where the bus stopped abruptly and Paddy Ryan yelled, "Get da fook out, before da light changes."

Out on the street it was cool but refreshing, as the young men buttoned up their blazers and headed for Old Abbey road. People were pouring onto the cobbled streets from every angle, as they headed to work with coats buttoned tight. On their way to the small apartment, Peter's silence stirred Thomas to say, "Don't worry my friend…the Immaculate Heart of Mary Church is not far, if you feel you're going to stray away." Peter grinned and replied, "I'm okay, it's just so exciting to be in this nice old city. I'm just little overwhelmed, that's all." Thomas playfully slapped him on the back and said, "Well, don't worry old bud, we'll find everything we're looking for right here."

After the guys had dropped off their bags, they began to settle in and plan their first day in Dublin city. Browsing the local map, Peter suggested, "How about the Glasnevin Cemetery Museum?"

"That's kind of dead Peter, I have a better plan than that my dry friend…"

"What did you have in mind?"

"Let's go over to St. James's Gate."

"To a church?"

Thomas laughed, grabbed his hat and said, "It's the Guinness Storehouse at St. James's Lane. The best beer on the planet."

"I don't know Tom…we're studying to be priests…"

"Well, that doesn't mean we have to be monks. Grab your hat old chap and let's grab a pint of Guinness."

Within minutes, the young men were down to the O'Connell Bridge and waiting for the bus to take them along the Liffey, over to St. James's Gate. On the way over, the activity of hustle and bustle could be seen in all directions, as the bus slowly snaked along the riverbank near the Victory Quay. With one quick bus transfer, they were soon headed up towards the Guinness brewery with a new thirsty perspective.

Down at the Guinness brewery, the black beer bottles lined the conveyor belts as far as the eye could see. Like soldiers in waiting, the renowned brew stood proudly upon the shiny shelves, ready to provide shelter from the front lines of everyday life. With the completion of a short tour of the brewing facility provided by the knowledgeable facilitator, Thomas and Peter sat back in the tasting room and waited for the heavy-handed beer. Without delay, an older woman arrived with two beers, banged them on the table and said, "There ya go lads, the first is on the house, da rest is on you…"

"Cheers Peter!"

"Cheers!"

"Now…isn't this better than a stiff old graveyard?"

"I have to admit, the beer is pretty good."

The smooth tasting beer went down easier, each time the old woman banged the brew upon the big brown table. One beer led to another, until too many brews had been consumed by the two polluted priests. In a slanted state of numbness, Thomas called out, "I believe our glasses are dry, Madam."

"And that's how they'll stay laddie. We're close'n now, so get yer arses move'n."

The fresh air struck them like the stones that lined the dark misty streets of old Dublin city. While they willingly poured the black luscious liquid down their hatch, night had arrived and with it, the opportunity to partake in a full-fledged pub crawl. Stumbling back and forth under the dim street lanterns, Peter noticed the determined glaze upon his stupefied friend. He may have had too many beers, but he still had sense enough to stop Thomas's run-a-way intentions of continuing on. Before Thomas could formulate a plan, Peter yelled to the passing car, "Taxi!"

Thomas wiped his face and slurred, "My good man…the night has just started…"

"And now it has ended for us, Tom."

"But we should have fun before our freedom is taken from us."

"Is that what you think, Tom? Our freedom is going to be taken…"

On a night when all reasonable questions were wasted to the wind, Thomas's response came with a gushing flow of brown beer and a well digested meal. He was too sick to answer any complicated questions and they both were too drunk to continue without the assistance of a Dublin cabbie.

The sounds of the midday city finally stirred the reluctant residents on Old Abbey Street. Unaccustomed to alcohol, they both were beyond the quick repair of a customary Irish breakfast severed by the local landlady. Peter was the first to drag himself out of bed and answer the loud knock upon his door. As he slowly opened the door an old lady with a tray of cooked breakfast blared out, "Now bucko, it's time ya gets yer arses out of bed. I'm not run'n a halfway house here you know…"

Too sick to carry on a conversation or to defend himself, all Peter could say was, "Yes, ma'am."

"It's midday and ye sling shits are only getting up. Ya should be ashamed of yerselves…"

"Yes, ma'am…"

"Well…Get this in ya…And ya will feel better."

"Yes, ma'am…"

As one door slammed shut, the other door opened and out came bushy headed Thomas wearing the same clothes, as the night before. The landlady had come and gone like a tornado, leaving the shattered men with the echo of her booming voice and a tray of baked beans mixed with chopped potatoes.

"How's your head, Peter?"

"What head?"

"You have to admit, Peter…it was fun…"

"And that's enough of that, Tommy boy."

Thomas flashed a wide grin and said, "For now…"

Peter picked up the tray, placed in the middle of the small table, and said, "I have a different plan for today…"

"And what might that be?"

"First we'll get our stomachs nourished with this breakfast and then we'll have our souls cleansed by our brothers."

"Cleansed?"

"Yes, we'll make a visit to the St. Mary's Pro Cathedral."

"But…we're on holiday…"

"In our profession, there are no holidays, my friend."

The priest at St. Mary's Cathedral could not ignore the two young men wearing dark sunglasses and dressed like proper gentlemen. As they walked through the tall pillars, he went to them and said, "Welcome to the Pro. I'm Father O'Malley."

The warm welcome within the pristine pillars of the entrance did not remove the previous stains of guilt from the night before. To ensure their dark night of drinking too many brews would not find the ears of St. Brennan's' College, it was previously agreed upon, that a veil of secrecy should be maintained. Peter bowed his head in respect and said, "Thank you, Father, we are tourists from across the pond and just dropping in for a visit." Father O'Malley stared at the heavy shaded glasses and replied, "Glad you lads could join us for service…But there's just one thing…" He glanced in the direction of Thomas, and asked, "Do I know you from somewhere?"

"No, Father."

"Oh…you look familiar. Please, come into our church."

With a quick glance at each other, the disguised seminary students walked into the historic cathedral behind the inquisitive priest. Within the vestibule and with the full echo of the building, the priest sharply pivoted around, and quickly asked again, "Are you sure we didn't meet?" Startled by the priest's quick action and rattled by the reoccurring question, Thomas said in a shaking motion, "No, Father, I'm sure we have never met before."

Peter quickly grabbed Thomas's coat when the priest turned around and franticly whispered, "I know him!"

"How?"

"He was at the College last year for a presentation."

"Holy cow…you're right…I remember now…"

Once again, the priest stopped in his steps. This time, he put his finger confidently in the air, spun around and said nothing. The two shaded young men had disappeared without giving him the third opportunity of interrogation. From the slamming of the church door, Father O'Malley wouldn't know, who the pale-faced young men were and why they left in such a hurry.

Outside, on the safety of the sidewalk, Peter and Thomas had finally caught their breath from a short but quick sprint. Still recovering from the Guinness, the green-gilled men gasped for air, as they swayed upon the cobbled stones. Peter shook his head and breathlessly said, "Boy, that was close…"

"Naw…He didn't have a clue who we were."

"Do you doubt everything, Thomas?"

"I think we both have doubt."

Thomas's doubting statement hit its reluctant target with staggering accuracy. Without knowing it, his sobering words of truth struck a soft nerve. Peter had been teetering back and forth for years but with the stark reality of those simple words, everything became unraveled right before his sick eyes.

On the rocky road of Dublin, with nothing but doubt and uncertainty in his mind, Peter had become lost. Just in the time of personal weakness, as his faith was faltering, a young woman stepped out of the shadows with a tempting proposal. With a stack of tickets in her hand, she seductively pointed out, "My, my, what a couple of strap'n lads you are…"

Thomas quickly replied, "We're not buying what you're selling Ma'am."

"I'm not yer fook'n Ma'am and I'm not sell'n fook'n anything."

Thomas politely responded, "Sorry…we didn't mean…"

"No worries lad. I'm not selling anything, but I'll give ya two tickets for free."

Realizing the mess he had already placed Peter in, Thomas looked at the young woman and said, "Thank you, but I think we already had enough excitement for one day." Out of the blue and to Thomas's amazement, Peter piped up and asked, "What are the tickets for?"

"That's me lad! Here's two tickets for da Temple Bar."

She quickly handed over the tickets and slipped off into the shadows of night, leaving them with one last, "Ye'll get what yer look'n for…Down at da Temple…"

Thomas stared at Peter with wonder, knowing of his friend's previous reluctance to enter the world of temptation. He slowly took the ticket from Peter and said, "I didn't think this was your cup of tea…"

"When you said I had doubt…it struck me hard."

"I didn't mean to question your faith, Peter."

"Well, I'm glad you did, Tom."

"Why?"

"Because maybe I'll find answer, down at the Temple Bar."

The red shiny building shimmered off the wet cobble stones in front, beckoning the men in from the cool evening mist. People from far and wide were leaning, sitting and standing in every nook and cranny of the bar. Warmly lit colors of red, green and brown welcomed all shapes and sorts of every kind. It was, indeed, a place where anyone could let their hair flow and leave their guard down. Under the glow of the warm lights, Peter and Thomas were slightly startled when a young waitress said in a sharp tone, "What'll it be b'ys?"

"Aww…not Guinness…"

"Ya have a problem with Irish beer then!"

"No…No…we had too much last night…"

"Well Jameson whiskey it is!"

The pretty young waitress stared into the eyes of Peter for a moment, then she was off behind the bar to pour the whiskey. Thomas noticed the flush on Peter's face, and said, "She's attractive, hey…"

"I like the warm feeling in here Tom, reminds me of home."

At the other side of the bar, a brown eyed admirer caught the eye of Thomas, causing him to stutter, and say, "I…I…have a warm felling in this bar too…"

Her sky-blue eyes within inches of his face, startled Peter and sent his head sharply back. She laughed and said, "I didn't think I was that scary."

Embarrassed by his involuntary reflexes, the red-faced Peter replied, "Oh…you're not scary…You're very pretty."

She laughed again and said playfully, "And now you're try'n to come on to me. Try'n a bit of Irish luck, are we?"

"No…Honestly I was…"

"My name is Katie O'Reilly…and ya never know yer luck if ya don't try."

The pretty young blue-eyed woman laid the drinks down and left with Peter watching her and Thomas drooling over the brown-eyed bartender. Thomas put his glass towards Peter and said, "Here's to Ireland!"

As the evening wore on and the whiskeys kept coming, they were once again, feeling no pain. With their inhibitions disabled by the premium whiskey, the parameters of conversation slowly became distorted and beyond the point of salvation. Peter had become lost in the sky-blue eyes of the Irish beauty and Thomas had been found by the brown-eyed bartender. One by one, the tables were losing the company of their companions, until there was only a single table remaining with one sole person. Katie O'Reilly sat down beside Peter and said, "Don't look so sad Peter Malone…your friend is in good hands."

Peter glanced over at Thomas standing too close to the brown-eyed bartender, and said, "You don't understand…"

"What I know is…his name is Johnny Black and he's a good lad."

"I'm sure he is but what you don't know is…"

Just as he began to tell her of their hidden profession, Thomas flashed a quick wave, and he was out the door with Johnny Black. Katie laughed, waved at Johnny and said, "Looks like someone will get da Irish luck tonight."

"Pardon me?"

"Can't you see? They're both as gay, as two jay birds."

"But he's studying to be a priest…"

"He'll be studying Johnny Black pretty soon."

Peter was suddenly sober, as he looked at the pretty young waitress and said, "This was all a mistake…"

Katie O'Reilly rose to her feet and sharply said, "Well I'm not a fook'n mistake Peter Malone…"

He quickly grabbed on to her arm and said, "No…no…I didn't mean that…"

"What did you mean?"

Peter released her arm and said, "We…are both studying to be priests…"

Katie O'Reilly sat back down, took a sip of his whiskey and said, "I won't hold dat against ya Peter Malone."

Chapter 11

Crossroads of Confusion

Outside the Temple bar it was colder than expected, prompting Peter to remove his jacket and place it over Katie's shoulders. She smiled, and said, "I'm only a couple of streets away…You really don't have to walk me home, if ya don't want to."

"I would love to walk you home, Katie O'Reilly."

Through the evening mist they walked and talked in rhythm with motion of the fast-flowing River Liffey. Katie's sharp mind and quick wit had Peter in a captivated trance. He had never been so close to a woman, who moved him so much. Unexpected feelings grew with every step Peter took and each moment he looked upon her smiling Irish eyes. When they reached Usher's Quay, Katie pointed up the road and said, "I'm just up here, off Island Street…" For the next few minutes, the conversation had stalled, until Katie suggested, "Why don't ya come in for a wee drink, Peter Malone…"

"I don't know, I'm worried about Tom."

"Oh…don't worry about him…dat fella will get jammy tonight…"

"Excuse me?"

"He'll be fine."

Peter stopped, looked out towards the swift moving Liffey and said, "I didn't expect things would happen like this…"

"Well, you never know when an opportunity will knock on your door."

"Is that what's happening with my friend Thomas?"

"Look here Peter Malone…he is where he is, because he wants to be." She took a step closer to Peter and continued, "Where do you want to be?" Peter took the key from her hand, opened the green door and walked in behind her.

That night, the rain poured down hard and pounded on the tile roof of Katie O'Reilly's old house. Under the protection of those rock tiles, the sweet release of restrained love flowed throughout the night. With Katie's tender touch, Peter Malone had taken a step through a forbidden green door he would never forget. As morning came and the rain subsided, Katie waited until Peter opened his eyes, "You didn't learn that in seminary school…"

"I didn't know what I was doing…"

"You're not too bad Peter Malone…for a priest…"

"I'm not a priest yet."

"Don't worry, you'll get yer wings, Peter."

"I believe myself and Tom have broken wings, as of last night…"

"You guys were just blow'n off some steam. Ye'll be alright."

"I have to check on him."

"He's at yer apartment, with Johnny."

"How do you know?"

"Johnny told me last night."

"How did you know I would stay here?"

"By your hungry eyes…"

"This was wrong…"

Katie jumped out of bed and stood with her hands on her hips. With a spitfire look, she sharply said, "If it was that wrong, then leave. Or stay with me, for the right reasons." Peter shut Katie's green door and headed out over the wet stones, determined to find out where he stood with Thomas Barker.

Peter opened the door of the apartment and slowly walked into the main room. Within seconds, Thomas walked out of his bedroom and sat down on the wooden chair. In the darkened room their eyes never focused, as they began to address what never happened. Thomas stood up, went to the stove and put the kettle on. He stared at the kettle, and said, "I think it would be best if I stay here until it's time to go back…" The presence of a person in Thomas's bedroom prompted Peter to respond, "Okay, I'll stay somewhere else." Thomas took two cups from the cupboard and without looking at Peter, he asked, "Would you like some tea?" Peter shook his head, and replied, "I'll meet you down at the O'Connell bridge bus stop in two weeks." Thomas poured out the two cups of tea, looked towards the bedroom door, and said, "You know Peter, we don't have to be celibate until we become priests." Peter stood, opened the door and replied, "It may be too late to worry about that Tom…"

Outside the shiny green door, Peter waited in the cool air and watched while people crossed the bridge over the

Liffey. Katie O'Reilly finally opened the door, "What took ya so long, Peter Malone?" Katie quickly prepared a light lunch and as they sat down to eat, she smiled said, "Don't worry Malone, I'll take good care of ya."

Peter grinned and replied, "And that's what I'm worried about…"

"Don't worry yer holy head. We'll have some fun for da next two weeks."

"If my mother could only see me now…"

"Well, she's not here and I am…So let's worry about today."

Peter nodded his head took a mouthful of lunch, and said, "You're a good cook…"

She struck him on the leg and said, "I'm good at other things too." Peter lifted his eyebrows, quickly stirred his spoon and straightened his back. She playfully laughed and continued, "I'm good at showing people around this city too."

In a limp state, Peter said, "I'd like that."

"Well, get that grub in ya…and we'll go for a dander."

At two in the afternoon, the O'Connell Bridge was fairly busy with people coming and going over the river Liffey. It was a beautiful blue-sky in Dublin and with every step they took, Peter was becoming more comfortable with Katie O'Reilly's Irish brogue. She knew everything about Dublin and wasn't afraid to pour out some spicy adjectives along the way to add Irish flavor. Proudly, she would point in every direction and explain the history and the importance of her beautiful Dublin city. Just as they arrived at Trinity College, Katie pointed towards the gate and said, "That's where the famous Oscar Wilde went to college…"

Peter stopped, and said, "Ah…Tom's favorite writer…"

Katie added, "And Johnny's…"

Katie quickly pointed over to a bronze statue across the road, and exclaimed, "There she is!"

"Who?"

"Da, one and only Molly Malone…That's who!"

As they moved closer to the statue Peter began to admire the intricate bronze work of the artist. Katie put her hands on her hips and buoyantly asked, "Did ya ever see a set of knockers like that Peter Malone?"

The big bosomed bust of Molly Malone was not hard to miss, but Peter replied, "What are you referring to?"

"Go on Peter…You know exactly what I mean…"

He slipped out a smiled and said, "She's a very healthy woman indeed."

Katie flicked her head back and replied, "Yer just gaffin' with me…" Then jumped upon the base of the statue and began to sing, "*In Dublin fair city, where the girls are so pretty…*" With no backup from Peter, she skipped a few verses and started again, "*She died of a fever, and no one could save her…*" Still no response from the tight-lipped Peter, until she shouted, "Finish it ya melter…"

Peter sat down and in low voice, he sang, "And that was the end of sweet Mary Malone…"

"Mary Malone? It's Molly Malone ya hallion!"

"I know, but my mother's name is Mary Malone…"

"Well, good fer her."

"I wonder, what she would think of me now…"

"She's not here and she can go get her own cockles and mussels for all I care."

"That wasn't called for…"

Realizing she had taken it too far, Katie sat beside Peter and softly said, "I'm just have'n a craic with me fella, that's all."

"It's okay, I know you were only having fun…it's not your problem…" Katie gently kissed him on the cheek and said, "It's my problem now…"

In the best of his ability, Peter explained about his expedited path to priesthood. He began from the beginning, when had been marked by his adoring mother to have a greater purpose. Peter told of her continual push to priesthood at any and all cost. Somewhere along the way, his own thoughts had become distorted and mingled into producing one common dream. But as time went on, the fine line of reality had faded to the point, where he didn't know his own path in life. Katie looked upon his torn face and said, "I'm sure your mother meant well for you, but it was her path and not yours."

"Maybe this is my path."

Katie took his hand, stood up and said, "Come on…I got something to show you…"

Off they went, down on Grafton Street, until they took a sharp right on Fleet Street. Katie was kicking up her heels at full pace, when Peter dragged her back down and asked, "Why the rush, Katie?"

"You'll see when we get there." They continued up Fleet Street and took a right turn towards the Liffey. As they ran, Peter shouted, "I'm wore out!" Katie laughed and said, "You didn't say that last night, Peter Malone." She continued to walk briskly toward the river, encouraging him as she went. Out on Wellington Quay Katie finally stopped, pointed up and exclaimed, "There she is!"

"Who?"

"The lovely Ha'Penny Bridge, that's who."

Right in front of them was the Liffey Bridge, affectionally known as the Ha'Penny Bridge. With its bright white exterior and beautiful arched form, it was an inviting opportunity to cross over the River Liffey in style. Katie stepped upon the cast iron pedestrian bridge, and said, "Come on, Malone…we'll cast yer troubles away." They got to the middle of the bridge where Katie stopped Peter with her two extended arms, and said, "Here." She placed a coin in his hand and continued, "Close yer eyes and make a wish, Peter Malone." Peter smiled, took the penny and closed his eyes.

For a moment in time, everything seemed to be perfect. The warm breeze upon his face and the smell of Katie's perfume lingered in his thoughts. As he paused in wonder, Katie chimed in, "Stop faffin' about, and just throw da penny." Peter smiled and threw the penny into the swift flowing Liffey. With his eyes still shut tight, he had wished time would stop right on the Liffey Bridge, when nothing seemed wrong and everything seemed right. Peter opened his eyes to find Katie two inches from his face. She quickly kissed him upon the lips, causing him to laugh uncontrollably in the middle of the Liffey River. At the height of his happiness, they warmly embraced and watched the deep water pass them by, as it made its way back to the open sea.

As the two remaining weeks soaked by, the undercurrent of uncertainty had not diminished or failed to flow. Peter never imagined he would be in a position, where uncharted choices had to be made upon the conclusion of his sabbatical. The new dimension of a relationship was not something he calculated or considered when he stepped off the bus three weeks ago.

In the shadow of the Temple bar, Peter waited outside for Katie while she finished her shift. Under the bright red building, he looked for answers from above but found only noisy patrons coming and going. Peter realized, he needed a safe place, where he could put back the pieces of his scrambled mind. Looking over across the river, Peter remembered a familiar place, where peace could be found in the quietness of his soul.

On the steps of St. Mary's Cathedral, Father O'Malley noticed Peter immediately. He walked over to him and asked, "Where's your Hollywood glasses?"

"You knew us…"

"Not right away, but when I remembered you from the seminary school I turned around and you guys had disappeared." Noticing the long face and the sad tone, Father O'Malley asked, "Do you want me to take your confession, laddie?"

"I believe, I'm beyond a confession."

"Well, I'd be da judge of that… Come into the St Mary's Pro, son."

Under the dome, Father O'Malley sat down on a pew and beckoned Peter to sit beside him. He asked, "Now what has happened that cannot be undone?"

"I have crossed the line of celibacy and I have drunk freely from the fountain of your Irish Guinness."

"Well, is that it, my son?"

"Father…I don't know if priesthood is for me…"

Father O'Malley gave Peter a slow Irish wink, and said, "I was a fresh-faced sheep farmer from Cork not too long ago and I too, lost my path along the way." He leaned back on the pew, unbuttoned his collar and explained, "Look…Plenty of water has flowed under the River Liffey since the time I started my spiritual journey, and I have realized we all go down wrong river sometimes. It is meant to be…It makes us stronger…We are just men of flesh and blood…Men make mistakes of every kind." Father O'Malley looked at Peter straight in the face and asked, "If we didn't make mistakes, how could we learn Peter?" The good priest put his hand upon Peter's shoulder, and continued, "I don't know if you are priest material. Only you will know that in yer heart…" He looked down upon the floor and said, "With regards to your romp in the hay. Well, that's something you have to reconcile within yourself. The love between man and woman is sacred, but if you want to be a priest, you must choose one or the other, my son." Just before Peter could reply, Father O'Malley quickly added with a sideways grin, "As for the drink'n from our renowned Irish fountain, well, I still partake in a few Guinness every now and again…and may God forgive me for that."

Peter gave his new mentor a slight smile that quickly dissipated when he continued, "But there is more, Father…" By the look upon the seminary students face, Father O'Malley rebuttoned his collar and said, "Continue…"

"Back home in our parish many despicable events happened at the hands of few priests."

"I see…"

In that old Cathedral, with its history of controversy, Peter went on to tell a distorted tale of demented actions that took the lives of Mark Godfrey and Kevin Callum. The old priest's pain could not be hidden, as river of tears ran down his wrinkled Irish face. He swallowed hard with every word Peter spoke, knowing the dark waters were deeper than they both really knew.

In the absence of the bigger silence, Father O'Malley sadly said, "Your parish is not alone."

With great sadness the old priest explained, "There is an understanding that there are ones who mingle among us, that wear the sacred cloth but not its meaning. They are wolves in sheep's clothing, who are attempting to destroy the fabric of our holy cloth..." Father O'Malley stood in the sanctuary of his stone Cathedral, and finished, "We must be strong...You must be strong Peter, to push them back into the depths of hell." In the company of Father O'Malley, Peter realized what he had to do. Invigorated with a new mission of salvation for his parish, he walked out, cleansed of his sins and ready to finish what he had started.

Peter opened Katie's green door and found her leaning over the stove stirring a steaming pot. She smiled, and asked, "Where did you go? I came out from the bar and you disappeared..."

"I went to see the priest over at St. Mary's..."

She continued to stir the pot, and softly asked, "Did you become enlightened?"

"You know...I have to go back..."

Katie was well aware of the date and the time, when Peter would reunite with his friend Thomas Barker. She knew from the beginning it was only for fun and it would be all gone like the water that flowed under the Liffey River. She also understood the price she would pay for falling in love with a priest. Katie O'Reilly understood extremely well, if she really loved Peter, she would have to set him free. Katie turned the stove burner off, and said, "I have a gift for you, Peter Malone."

From a simple brown paper bag, Katie removed a bright green sweater that had Ireland embroidered proudly on the front. She placed it in on his chest, and with a smile on her face and tears rolling down her cheek, she said, "What do ya know…it fits ya perfect…"

At the bus stop, they waited for Thomas Barker, but he did not appear. Peter could see Paddy Ryan's big yellow bus coming from the distance and knew, the time had expired for Tom and had ended for his beautiful Katie. She quickly kissed him on the cheek and left him with a key and the words, "If ya comes to Dublin again…I'll be here for ya." Paddy Ryan quickly pulled up on the sidewalk, opened the door and shouted, "Get da fook in, before da light changes."

Chapter 12

Stumbling Onward and Upward

Peter walked down the hallowed hall of the college and right to his room without stopping to speak with anyone. There was only one person he needed to see, who understood the feeling of loss he felt at that moment. Somehow, he believed Thomas Barker had miraculously made his way back into their room and was waiting for his return. The reality soon struck Peter when he opened the door to his room and found a stranger sitting on Thomas Barker's bed. Stephen welcomed him back, and said, "This is Bruce Barrow, our new roommate."

Later, when the formality of the introduction and small talk had subsided, Peter signaled Stephen outside. The two men never spoke, until they reached the sanctuary of the chapel and isolation from the oak doors. In the apparent rush to get Stephen in the privacy of the chapel, Peter became strangely silent. He had plenty to say but didn't know how to begin. Stephen anticipated the hesitation and Peter's reluctance to speak, so he began, "I see you guys have been busy during the sabbatical."

"Is Tom coming back, Stephen?"

"No, Peter, he gave notice to Father Kelly..."

"I think we overstepped our boundaries, Stephen."

"That's something you will have to decide."

"Did you know Tom was gay, Stephen?"

"It was never my business to know..."

For some strange reason, Peter felt he should come clean with everything. Maybe it was the ambiance of the chapel, or maybe it was the sincerity of his friend, but at moment, it was time to confess it all. Peter blessed himself, and then started with the booze blast at the brewery and ended with the revelation of his relationship with Katie O'Reilly. Everything was completely laid out, even the fact that Thomas Barker had a fling with Johnny Black. With all the specifics laid upon the offertory table, Peter waited for Stephen to respond.

"Hmmm...That's a lot of information my friend."

"I'm not proud of it."

"Do you love Katie?"

"I don't know..."

"Why did you come back?"

"I don't know..."

"It seems like Thomas knew what to do."

"What do you think of his relationship, Stephen?"

"Who am I to judge?"

"Our colleges seem to judge it wrong."

Stephen stood from his pew and asked, "How can love be wrong, Peter?" He went over to the door, opened it and before he left, he said, "You better take a shower..."

"Excuse me?"

"I can smell Katie's perfume a mile away."

The door shut leaving Peter alone with his fresh memories. Three weeks had come and gone in a city where the river flowed, and the love flourished. In the dim light of the chapel, Peter lit another candle of encouragement, as he prayed for strength he needed in the strong fragrance of her sweet memory.

Even though Stephen was a good friend, Peter missed the company of his funny companion. The remaining years passed by, without tomfoolery antics or his quick-witted comments. Even old Paddy Ryan missed the lad, who pushed his hot Irish temper and cocked his hair-triggered mouth. It had been a dull time without Thomas Barker's solid friendship and his comical relief, but he prevailed, and he finally made it to the ordained altar of priesthood.

On the last week of seminary school, during the pull of incoming students and the push of outgoing graduates, Peter realized his time in Ireland had come to an end. Even at his weakest point, when he stumbled at St. James's Gate, St. Brennan's College had been a lighthouse of hope in the choppy waters of River Liffey. It appeared everything worked out just the way it should, but for some reason, there was something still missing from his life. When Peter began packing his bag, he picked up the missing link to his happiness and placed it on the bed. The intoxicating scent of Katie O'Reilly's perfume, still lingered on the bright green sweater she gave him. Peter picked it up, placed in his suitcase and headed to the phone room down the hall.

In the noisy Temple Bar, Katie O'Reilly answered the phone. "Hello…" Peter did not respond, he just stood with the receiver in his hand and a lump in his throat. "Hello…Peter, is that you?" Only the hard swallow of his desperate silent plea could be heard. Katie finally said, "I love you, Peter Malone." Peter replied, "I love you too, Katie O'Reilly…" With the true confession of those words, he hung up the receiver and went on to prepare for his final departure.

It was dark and cold, when Paddy Ryan picked up Peter's bag and placed it in the trunk of the car. Peter sat in the front seat wearing a hard black suit, topped off with a stiff white collar. Paddy turned the key, pivoted his head towards Peter and said, "You're look'n some fook'n sharp this morn'n, Father Malone." Peter grinned at Paddy and affectionately replied, "Don't ever change, Paddy."

On the flight back home, Peter could feel the influence of his black attire from the comforting smiles and the respecting nods of the passengers. Unaccustomed to his newfound fame, Peter felt out of place with the unearned adoration that they placed at his feet. Peter may have been fresh from the seminary college, but he had learned from his mother, the damage blind praise could invoke. He recalled her unwavering support for the guilty ones, even in the face of their unraveling fake facade. The new stiff white collar, which dug deep into his neck, reminded him to always guard against his own vanity. With his eyes closed tight, he prayed that he would cast out any future feelings that would put him ahead of those who were no more, or no less than him.

Seven hours later, the plane's deceleration signaled the conclusion of the flight and the beginning of his new life in the new world. Peter was well aware the challenge he faced and did not forget the task he needed to tackle. He quickly realized that his lack of seniority would place him in the back of the sacristy where his voice would be muted. Peter also understood, the task of facing his adversaries would position him in front of the Archdiocese crosshairs. The sharp screech of the landing wheels shocked his senses into realizing, he had finally arrived home, and it was time for a new spiritual reckoning.

The crowded celebration at the arrival gate did not take Peter by surprise. He was forewarned of his mother's ambitious plan of placing her newly minted priest on display for everyone to see. This expected exhibition was completely understood to be Mary Malone's heavenly reward for producing such a fine priest. It was her moment of glory and he was not going to take it away, even though he detested the spotlight of pomp and ceremony. In the sea of smiling familiar faces that came to welcome him home, Peter noticed a dark cloaked man who beckoned his attention. After the last handshakes and celebratory hugs, Peter went to the man and said, "You must be Father King…"

"It's nice to finally meet you, Father Malone."

"I'm sorry for the short introduction, Father King, but I'm leaving to go my parents for a celebration dinner."

"You don't understand Father Malone, I'm here to pick you up."

"But what about my family?"

"They'll have to wait…Bishop Stone is waiting to speak with you."

The sweet smell of pipe tobacco struck Father Malone with pleasant memory. He remembered his father's best friend, Father Piercy sitting in their shed. Between Gus Malone's newly cut shavings and Father Piercy's freshly stoked pipe, the smell had embedded a time of peace and tranquility. From a high lofted ceiling at the Bishop's residence, Bishop Stone's voice cut through Peter's silent thoughts, when he unknowing shouted, "Where the blue blazes is that man?"

Father King cleared his throat loudly and gently tapped on the post outside Bishop Stone's mahogany door. He softly entered and said, "Uh-umm…Father Malone is here."

Somehow, the Bishop looked smaller than he remembered so many years ago. Back then, he thought the Bishop was an imposing figure with a booming voice and a demanding presence. Now, under the cloud of pipe smoke, he could see nothing but a small bent man with high-pitched voice and demeaning disposition. Of course, his bias stance had been galvanized by the treatment of his friend Father Truman. In the assurance of politeness and respect, Father Malone placed out his hand and said, "It's a pleasure to meet you Bishop Stone." Ignoring the extended hand, the Bishop scanned the new priest from head to toe and then placed his ring finger out to be kissed.

Within the mahogany walls of books and brass fittings, Peter sat in the leather chair at the foot of Bishop Stone's solid oak desk. After another short silence, the Bishop got down to business, by stating, "We expect obedience within the ranks of our priests."

"Of course, your Excellency…"

"I will not tolerate any insolence for disobedience."

"Of course, your most Reverend."

"I will not accept any insubordination from my subordinates."

"Of course, your most Reverend, Excellency…"

Bishop Stone began to relax, by the quick agreeable responses from his new priest. He opened the oak desk drawer, placed a freshly printed document in front of Father Malone, and said, "This package has all the details regarding your new parish."

"Thank you, your Excellency."

"You will be pleased to know that I have assigned you in your home parish."

"Thank you, your most Reverend."

"I believe you knew the former parish priests, Father Piercy and Father McKnight."

"And Father Truman, your most Reverend Excellency."

The Bishop could not hide the scowl of disgust upon his crumpled face. He quickly changed the subject, with a quick, "Don't speak of his name again." The stale stuffy air within the confines of stained walls could be cut with a knife. Peter could taste the small trickle of blood oozing from his lip, as he replied with the nodding of his head.

"Also…you must show your congregation, who the boss of the parish is."

"Yes, your Excellency."

"They have old stained-glass windows in the church…"

"Yes, your most Reverend."

"You will remove them and replace them with new modern windows…as a sign of control…"

Peter knew those stained-glass windows well. He had seen his Grandfather hand carve them with the help of many hands from the parish. Those beautiful windows were the pride and joy of everyone in their parish and all who laid their eyes upon the hand-crafted beauty.

He answered Bishop Stone's strong suggestion, with an intentional, misdirected question. "May I join my family in our celebratory dinner, your most Reverend Excellency?" The Bishop went to the door, held out his pasty ring finger and said, "I will be watching you, Father Malone."

Father Malone opened the screen door of the parish house and walked into his familiar new home. As a child, he would play in and around that old house, while his father talked for hours with his best friend. He remembered Father Piercy's friendly face and his gentle tone of understanding no matter what circumstances were laid upon their table of conversation. Those pleasant memories had been engraved into the fabric of his mind, as he soaked in his new reality of being a priest, in his own parish.

Peter unpacked his clothes, went downstairs and hung his bright green sweater upon a hook in the dark hall. Placing the kettle on the stove, he recognized a familiar voice coming from the front screen door. Peter quickly shouted, "Come in Pat, the door is opened."

Pat Morey walked into the kitchen and said, "Welcome home, Father Malone." With a warm handshake, Father Malone said, "It's good to be home, Pat." Pat Morey sighed and said, "You don't know how much we missed you here…"

"When did Father McKnight leave, Pat?" Pat Morey's pleasant smile quickly turned upside down. He looked out through the window and went suddenly quiet. Father Malone picked up on the common vein of contention and guided the conversation quickly away. He asked, "How have you been, Pat?"

Pat Morey regained his composure and replied, "I'm okay…"

Noticing Pat's demeanor was still distracted he continued to ask, "How's is your son Justin doing?"

The whistle from the boiling kettle and Pat Morey's distressed situation, signaled the tea was ready to be poured. The gloomy room became darker when Pat broke down in front of the new priest. With hands shielding the tears of pain, he sobbed and said, "I knew Father Blake and Father Sable were bad…but I had no idea Father McKnight was worse…"

"What happened, Pat?"

"When Father Blake and Father Sable were moved to other parishes, I took this maintenance job on…I thought, with me working on the church premises…nothing could happen…I believed the rumors about abuse was only related to the two other priests…I was wrong…"

"Oh my God! Our worst fears came true, Pat." Pat Morey removed the hands from his face, to reveal a stream of tears and a gaping gouge of pain that could never be healed.

"We will bring him to justice…I promise…"

"I'm not an educated person Father Malone, but I'm smart enough to know…you can't fight the Archdiocese. Their pockets are deep, and their power is undisputed."

"Where's Justin?"

"Ever since the incident, just after you went to Seminary College, Justin has gone down a road of drugs and alcohol. There was nothing I could do but watch him destroy himself."

"Where is he?"

"Still at our house, living in the basement."

"I need to go there now…"

Five hard years of theology and philosophy was about to be tested only after twenty-four hours of landing back in his home parish. The blood pounded in his veins, as they hurried to the Morey's broken home with the thought of another childhood friend destroyed by the three priests of darkness. In that moment, Peter had realized, he had arrived home too late. Father McKnight had laid his hands on his friend Justin Morey, and now there was only one recourse. No matter what the cost, he would carry on where his best friend, Father Andrew Truman, had finished.

In the dark shaded basement, Peter found Justin rocking to heavy metal music with thick padded headphones. He was isolated from the rest of the world in confines of the Morey basement and insulated from the sound of his own mind by the constant pounding of the deafening beat. From a slice of light coming from the constricted window, Peter's frame cast a shadow of darkness upon the Justin's wall. Justin shuddered for a moment, and then recognized Peter's smiling face. Justin removed the headphones from his ears and said, "It's been a long time…I've been waiting for you…"

In the darkened room below ground level, words could not portray the pain that emanated from the fallen face of Justin Morey. It was not until the newly minted priest was in front of the man who wore scars of a young boy, that the true impact of devastation struck the soul of Peter Malone. The guilt he felt, for leaving Justin in the hands of the three cloaked wolves could not be easily diminished with a casual conversation. They left the small talk to the wind and began to relive the unspoken truth.

"What happened, Justin?"

"When you left for college, we all believed the presence of my dad would provide safety. While Dad worked around the property, keeping an eye on Father Sable and Father Blake, he left Father McKnight to his own devices." Father Malone sat down on the chair alongside Justin and put his head down. The young man continued, "In broad daylight and under the eyes of a community blinded by priestly bullshit, Father McKnight took advantage of me."

While still staring at the concrete floor, Father Malone said, "We thought the presence of your father would keep them at bay…I didn't realize the voraciousness of their appetite for the most vulnerable. We miscalculated…"

"Don't blame yourself for their actions, Peter…you were young then and didn't know."

"What can I do for you now?"

Justin placed the headphones down, stood up and said, "Take them to justice."

Father Malone grabbed Justin's two shoulders and replied, "I will not stop until they are taken from their parishes and brought to court."

"Bring the bastards to court, and I will try to carry on."

"I'll arrange a meeting with Bishop Stone when I leave here."

Justin Morey walked over to the small window, opened the shade a few inches and said, "If you fail, I can't go on any further…"

Peter knew there was no time to waste as he hurried back and called Father King for an urgent message. He hadn't been in the shoes of Father Truman and didn't know the frustration of what that man experienced, when he tried to open their eyes to the blatant abuse. With the phone in hand and with the image of his damaged friend seared into his mind, the reality of complication quickly became apparent, when he confronted a holy system that was hell bent on putting up barriers.

"But…Father King this is extremely important…"

"As I just explained, Bishop Stone is unable to meet with you in such short notice."

"You don't understand…it's a matter of life or death…"

"Are you saying someone is dying at this moment?"

"No…But…"

"Well, I suggest you call back tomorrow, and I'll provide a time in the future when he is available."

"That is not good enough."

"Look…Father Malone…Let me suggest this…The annual banquet for all priests in the Archdiocese next Monday. You may be able to get his ear at that time."

"But you don't understand…"

"No…you don't understand, it's the best I can do for you, Father Malone."

There was nothing left to do but wait until Monday would arrive and wonder if justice would prevail. Father Malone went to his parish church and looked upon the scaffolding that had been assembled in front of the old stained windows. Pat Morey happened to be cutting the grass out in front and quickly responded to Father Malone's beckoning wave. He pointed up at the scaffolding, and asked, "Why was that assembled?"

"Father King said you requested the windows to be removed."

"I didn't request them to be removed…"

"Didn't your grandfather hand carve them, Father Malone?"

He glanced around the vacant land, remembering the beautiful garden of lush trees with manicured bushes. It was a tranquil place, planted by the parishioners who carefully maintained it with love and affection. In failure to see what mattered to them, Father McKnight had cut it down in a display of power and control. Father Malone glanced up at the windows and then he looked at Pat Morey, and asked, "Please take that scaffolding down…"

"What will I do with the windows Father King ordered for you?"

"Send them to the dump…where they belong."

Just as Pat Morey began to walk off with a wide smile upon his face, Father Malone stopped him, and said, "Tell Justin to hang on…I'll have his answers on Monday."

Chapter 13

The Sacrificial Soul

On Monday morning, all the priests arrived at the Archdiocese headquarters for the annual banquet. The atmosphere was full of friendly interaction with plenty of jokes and good-natured teasing by priestly friends from every parish. Most of the priests were fully aware, that the banquet was only an excuse to get together for rest and relaxation. It was an annual time to get away from the strict protocol of the parish and kick up their heels in the company of the common cloth. For everyone who had entered the banquet hall, with the exception of one, it would be a special day of eating fresh lamb and sipping on old scotch.

As they filed into the great dining hall and began to settle in, Father Malone arrived without a smile or the desire to mingle. It was his first time attending this type of event and he wasn't aware that serious discussions or topics of concerns weren't encouraged. He didn't know that it was not a place, where life for death dilemmas were presented upon the table of fine dining.

Peter Malone was a gullible new priest, in an unfamiliar world where discontent was discouraged by all means. One of the older priests took the discontented demeanor of the newer priest as a sign of nervousness. He walked up to Peter and said, "You can leave your white collar at the door my new friend." He walked him into the dining hall to join three other priests standing by an overflowing table of refreshments. They all welcomed him in with a nod, and the friendly priest asked, "And what will you have Father, ah…"

"Peter…"

"Yes…what will you have, Father Peter?"

Father Peter quickly scanned the tables and noticed everyone there was drinking alcohol. Just to fit in he replied, "I'll have a beer please."

The four priests stopped sipping their glasses and one said with a grin, "No, my dear Father Peter…You are a full-fledged priest with a parish now."

Peter gave a fragile smile and said, "I don't understand…"

The priest placed a glass of straight scotch in Father Peter's hand and said, "You are in the scotch club now…You will drink only the best single malt scotch."

Before Father Peter could respond, Father King signaled to him from across the room. He excused himself and went to Father King and asked, "When will I get an opportunity to speak with Bishop Stone?"

"Well, that's the thing…I mentioned to the Bishop, that you had a concern and…"

"Yes…What did he say?"

"He told me, to tell you, under no circumstances are you to bring up anything pertaining to outside matters."

Peter's blood began to boil instantaneously. He quickly regained his thought process and asked, "What about Monsignor Murphy, can I speak with him?"

"Monsignor Murphy never attends these events. He doesn't like alcohol."

Again, Father Malone began to formulate another way. He asked, "Is there any chance to speak during the dinner?"

"There are toasts given after the conclusion of the meal, but it's only a limited opportunity for short compliments." Father Malone took the glass of scotch to his lips and with one gulp, he chugged it down. He lowered the empty glass, and said, "I'm ready to give a toast to Bishop Stone, that he may find hard to swallow."

Fine dining was not something Father Malone expected, when given the invitation on such a short notice. After arriving in his parish only a few days before and finding his parishioners suffering in silence, he was in no mood for small talk or any fancy meals. Father Peter had no appetite for freshly sliced lamb served on a silver platter. He pushed the full plate in front of him and sipped on his scotch, while he waited until his golden opportunity was given to him on an empty stomach.

On a table of spilled wine and wasted bread, expensive scotch seemed something hard for Peter to swallow. The bitter taste of opulence and the distorted look of lavishness made him realize, the fresh drink laid in front of him would be his last glass of expensive scotch.

At the head table Bishop Stone was flanked by Father Blake to the left and Father McKnight to the right. It was a sickening sight for a priest who knew the level of darkness they cast over the victims and their loved ones. He watched them casually banter, as if all was perfect under the safety of their bent Bishop. With his unanswered hand hanging in the air, Father Malone upped the stakes when he pushed back his chair and stood to the attention of all that were seated, "I have an announcement to make."

Bishop Stone was quick to respond by saying, "I believe your announcement can wait until a more suitable time."

"No, your most holy Excellency, it cannot wait…"

Father Malone quickly left his seating position at the back of the room and walked briskly to head table. In front of all the priests and a few feet away from the guilty perverts, the expensive white linen tablecloths were about to get stained.

Before Father Malone began to speak, Bishop Stone looked at the outspoken, new priest and said, "Father ah…"

"Malone."

"Yes, Father Malone if you're not giving a toast, please return to your seat. There will no discussions on any serious matters today."

"I'm afraid it's too late to take my seat, your Excellency…"

"And why is that, Father Malone?"

"It is a matter of life or death, for a young man who needs our support."

"Right now, it's a matter of you speaking out of line…Go back to you seat, Father Malone."

"I cannot go without knowing, that Father McKnight will be held accountable for raping the young boy from our parish…"

The word, raped, draped over the table and demanded every head to spin in the direction of a desperate priest.

Bishop Stone stood to his feet and with his flushed, fire-red face he shouted, "ENOUGH!"

What started out as a lavish event with small talk and laughter, ended up with an inadequate response by a stoned-faced Bishop. Priests from all parishes sat in shock, while they stared upon a new priest who had spoiled their hot lamb dinner with the cold hard truth. Under the strain of Father Peter Malone's accusation, a crack in the foundation of the Archdiocese began to appear. Bishop Stone had no intention of allowing that deep reaching crack to spread any further, when he pointed towards the door, and angrily said, "Outside."

Away from the reaching ears and inquisitive glances, Bishop Stone went down to the basement of the building, followed by Father Malone. When he was sure it was safe to be blunt, Bishop Stone faced Father Malone, and said, "You cannot make an accusation without sufficient evidence to back it up."

"I have the evidence…I have the word of a victim…"

"The word of a foolish young man against a priest?"

"He is telling the truth, Bishop Stone."

"HE doesn't know what truth IS!"

Bishop Stone struck his crumpled fist on his leg and with spray of frustration he said, "You fool…You have no idea, what damage you could invoke on the Archdiocese."

"Bishop Stone, this is a deeper problem. There have been other incidences of abuse by Father Sable and Father Blake…"

The Bishop fired over a sharp look and said, "We will handle all internal matters within the Archdiocese. There will be no more discussion of this…to anyone…"

"Bishop Stone, the other victims have died by suicide and I'm afraid this person will do the same unless we take it to the legal system."

Taking matters to court and flashing them in the front of the public, was not where Bishop Stone wanted to sink anytime soon. He was caught in a corner and realized a change of strategy was required to calm down the overemotional new priest, who could do irreparable damage to the Archdiocese's reputation and resources. With the legal costs tabulating in Bishop Stone's mind, he calmed down and tried a different approach, when he slyly suggested, "Go to him and tell him the Archdiocese is praying for him to be healed."

"This will not be enough…"

"Then…we will send an Archdiocese representative Father King, to speak with the young man."

"This will not do, Bishop Stone."

"Okay…we will send a team of priests to speak with his family. This will diffuse the situation."

"The time for talking with priests is over. It must be taken to the judicial system and revealed to the public."

The time for Bishop Stone's covert operation of sincerity had terminated, with the suggestion of the judicial system and the possibility of prying public eyes. His short fuse had been lit by a priest who had no time for a system that had lost its way. Red-faced Bishop Stone clenched his teeth, and bitterly said, "Your unwillingness to resolve a situation that has no merit and your pushback against our willingness to help, leaves me no choice but to relieve you of your parish."

"The faith of my position is not a concern of mine…You, turning your back on the victim is…"

"It was a mistake to trust you with the parish."

"It was a mistake to believe you would help us."

"Consider this your notice…you have one week remaining in your former parish."

"I don't care…"

"Oh…You'll care, when I send you where the sun doesn't shine…"

"Like the dark hole that you live in?"

Bishop Stone quickly turned his back on the sacked priest and scurried up the stairs to stanch the protection of his close supporters. Unfortunately for him, the strength of his support had been substantially weakened by a spoiled meal of sacrificial lamb. In the wake of Father Malone's revelation, the suspicion and rumors had been confirmed. In his short absence, immediate action had been taken by the direction of the majority. Father King had been given a directive of calling Monsignor Murphy back to the Archdiocese. They knew, the Monsignor may have had old fashioned ways and a strict disposition, but he would never support renegade priests who victimized his dearly beloved flock.

Alone in the basement of the Archdiocese, Father Malone was left with nowhere to go, but down to a dark place where the light of Justin Morey's soul was burning low. Without the support of his Bishop or the hope of a judicial solution, the dejected priest prepared to go back to his former parish empty handed.

Pat Morey had removed the scaffolding from the side of the church and was loading the unwanted new windows in the back of his truck, when Father Malone drove up in his car. Pat waited until the priest got out of his car, then he asked, "What do you really want me to do with these windows, Father?"

"Take them to the dump and smash them, before the new priest has any intention on removing our stained-glass relics." Automatically Pat Morey nodded his head in agreement but then he quickly realized, by the stark look upon his face that something was terribly wrong. Pat Morey stopped, and asked, "How did the meeting go?" Father Malone stood with his face into the sharp cold wind and never answered. His sunken eyes and fallen face were enough for Pat Morey to know, his son had been left to wolves and there was no hope for his salvation. Father Malone got back into his car, rolled the window and said, "I'm going to visit Justin…"

Justin had no intention of leaving his position in front of the stacked speakers. The heavy metal beat had carried him through tough times without judgment and drowned out memories of the past. Loud head banging music was his only release, from the constant reminder of the abuse he endured in the hands of Father McKnight. It was his lighthouse that kept him from drowning in his own thoughts, until Father Malone walked in and turned the music down. Justin removed his headphones and said, "You don't have to say anything, Peter…I can see it on your face…"

"Maybe in the future when the Bishop is replaced, there will be a chance, but right now, there is no way we can move forward."

Justin placed the headphone over his ears and closed his eyes. Father Malone turned down the volume, removed the headphones and said, "I will help you through this Justin."

"It's too late for help now, the music is almost over..."

"But we can do this together..."

"Nobody can walk in the steps of an abused person, unless you have been in their shoes...and I wouldn't wish that on anyone."

"But I can help you..."

"Yes, you can..." Justin placed the headphones and continued, "You can turn up the volume and leave..."

Father Malone walked up over the stairs to find Pat Morey waiting with dejected eyes and a desperate plea. He had heard their conversation and was unwilling to give up on a son who had been hurt on his watch. Pat stepped in front of the priest and suggested, "What if we go it alone, without the support of the Archdiocese and direct to the police?" Father Malone slowly nodded his head, and knowing it was a futile effort without the support of the Archdiocese, he said, "I'll be with you all the way..."

Under the circumstance of his short termination notice, Father Malone had intended on having a short mass without a long-winded sermon. This turned out to be more difficult than he expected, when he read the *sermon on the plain* from the gospel of Luke. When he spoke the words, "pray for the ones who abuse you," the pain could not be hidden from the congregation. Father Malone had unknowingly stopped and left the silence hanging upon the incense that permeated the air. In the absence of Father Malone's words, the light that had shone through the old stained-glass windows, was suddenly shaded by a dark cloud. The abrupt sign of darkness signaled it was time to move on and face the world with a different cheek and a new perspective.

Father Malone returned to the priest's house, and after a quick cup of tea in the kitchen, he walked upstairs to finish packing his suitcase. The climb to the top triggered senses he did not expect. It wasn't the reality of knowing that his times of walking upon those familiar steps were coming to an end. There was something else that didn't seem quite right, as he ascended the stairs and headed towards his lonely room at the end of the hall. With his hand on the doorknob, Peter realized by the smell of the blood, the pain had ended while the sun stopped shining through their beautiful stained windows.

In middle of the room, under a pool of blood and hanging from the light fixture by his stole, Justin Morey's misery had come to an end. The image was immediately seared into his soul, as he stood under the sight of Justin Morey's silent surrender. Hanging by the priests stole and cut by his own hand, the young man had ended his futile fight with a system that refused to acknowledge one of their own, had placed their hands upon his sacred body.

Father Malone gently took Justin's bloodied body down, with the help of his broken father, Pat Morey. They softly removed the blood-soaked stole and laid his peaceful corpse upon the white linen bed. While they waited in the room for the police, Pat Morey looked over at Father Malone and said, "This may sound cruel, but I'm glad my son's suffering is over."

"I didn't do enough for him, Pat…"

"You did everything you could, Father Malone…"

"It wasn't enough…"

"Where will you go, now that you have been removed from this parish?"

"My eyes were closed to the truth for so many years…and now for the first time, I can see, what I must do."

When the body was removed and silence had descended, Father Malone made a call to Father King to tell him about the deceased, Justin Morey. Father King had anticipated a call from the chastised priest about the parish transition but didn't expect the additional devastating news. The tragic news of the young man's death struck Father King extra hard. He had been in the great dining room, when Father Malone pleaded his case in front of a cold-hearted Bishop who was hell bent on silence. In reality of the new events Father King said, "His life will not be lost in vain."

"What do you mean by that, Father King?"

"There was movement among most of the priests when you left from the dining hall…and now with his tragic news…this will take it to a new level."

"It's too late Father King…but I would like to do the funeral mass before I leave."

"Absolutely…"

"I have one more request."

"Yes…"

"Could you invite my seminary friend, Father Stephen Easton to the service?"

"I will do my best to make it happen."

"Right now, he is the only one who can heal my soul."

Father Malone hung up the phone and went to clear his cluttered head, while he searched for the words of his homily. In the old church where the light streamed through the colored stained-glass windows, Peter fell to his knees. In a place that never failed to lift him up when he needed strength, he looked up at the altar and remembered his friend, Father Andrew Truman. He thought about the challenges his friend had faced and how he carried on, even when both of his parishes had been taken by Bishop Stone. At the point of remembering Father Andrew's selfless actions, Peter also remembered the words of wisdom he spoke. The words he needed for his homily, had come from a voice of his past and would serve as the light for his future.

Three days later the funeral service ceremony sadly commenced with family, friends and two supporting priests. In the front pew Pat Morey and his family could not be fully consoled, for the loss of their son was too great. They leaned upon each other for support and relied on Father Malone for strength to help with the never-ending pain. In the pew at the back of the church, Damian Malone sat with his face to the floor. His brother had called and given him the tragic news of their friend Justin Morey. Without delay, he returned to the parish in a show of solidarity for his brother and respect for the dearly departed. On the alter, Father Malone was joined by Father King on the left and Father Stephen on the right. Father King had placed pressure on the Archdiocese, and they approved the last-minute invitation for the foreign priest. Arriving hours before, Father Stephen had no idea of the tragic details. He only knew that Father Malone needed him, and he would not turn his back on a friend.

The mass moved on with the reverence and sadness expected for such a tragic event by the loss of such a young life. In Justin's last act of defiance, he gave up his life to send a strong sorrowful message for the lack of justice he was so sadly denied. Within the context of this somber mood, Father Malone performed the last mass in his home parish with a heavy heart, knowing there was a travesty of justice from the lack of embracing the truth. From the pulpit, he concluded the mass with a homily that revoked the absence of truth and invoked the embracing of truth. Father Malone had ended the funeral mass with a deep message that addressed the past and embraced the future.

When the service was over and Justin was laid to rest, Pat Morey went to the side of Father Malone as said, "At least he is at peace now…"

"Yes Pat, he died sending a strong message to those who wouldn't listen."

"Will there be any justice going forward, Father Malone?"

"I don't know, Pat…"

As Pat started to leave, Father Malone stopped him and asked, "Could you do me one more favor before I leave this parish?"

"Anything, Father Malone."

"Could you light a fire in that old barrel out behind the priest's house?"

"Of course, but why do you want a fire?"

"You'll know why, when the fire is raging…"

Chapter 14

The Burning Truth

"Peter…Peter…"

Deep within his mind, Peter Malone had walked through his past, as he stood in front of the burning fire. From the cradle of his mother's desire to position him on the path of priesthood to the final firing from his beloved parish, he had replayed his life while the flames of his burning vestments lifted to the heavens. Left with the bloodied stole clutched in his hands, Father Peter Malone stood under the close watch of Pat Morey and Father Stephen, as Damian repeated his name, "Peter…Peter…"

Peter Malone refocused his mind, stared at his brother, and searchingly said, "Damian…"

"Are you okay, Peter…you seemed to have left us for a while…"

"Yes, I'm fine…I was lost in the past."

"We wouldn't want to lose you now."

"I believe that I finally found my own true path." Damian placed his hand on Peter's shoulder and said, "I guess it's better late than never…"

Peter took the unintentional cue from his brother and tossed the blood-stained stole into the burning fire. Father Stephan blessed himself and said, "Your friend Justin is free...and in the arms of God..." Damian quickly added, "And your Bishop Stone and his three priests should be in the arms of the law."

Once again Father Stephen explained, "I don't know this Bishop Stone you speak of, or the three priests you mentioned...I only know of Bishop Murphy..."

From around the side of the house Father King appeared and came to the side of Father Stephen. He reached over to shake Pat Morey's hand and said, "We are with you." Damian flicked a stick into the fire barrel, and sarcastically said, "It's too late for empty promises from your Bishop Stone..." He stepped in front of Father King to finish, "Tell him to go Fuc..."

Before he could finish his surly suggestion, Peter stopped him with his hand in the air and said, "Find another job..."

When the fire slackened and Damian's temper had subsided, Father King gingerly said, "That's what I came to tell you. Bishop Stone was removed and replaced by Monsignor Murphy."

Father Stephen exclaimed, "Bishop Murphy is the one who sent for me!" Father King slowly nodded his head, and continued, "Bishop Murphy has called for a complete investigation into the three priests you named."

For a moment, they watched the fleeing embers from the blood-soaked stole as it danced upon the flames and lifted up towards heavenly sky. The heat from the hot fire barrel seemed to forge the reality that Justin Morey sacrificed his own life to stop the potential abuse of others. His final selfless act of protest had shone light on those who preyed on the innocent, under the pretense of praying priests.

The crackling from the burning wood at the bottom of the barrel, prompted Father King to say, "The new Bishop has indicted the problem may be deeper than what has been reported. His Reverence has indicted, there may be others that have slipped through the system due to their unwillingness to accept the reality of evil." In the light of the fire, Peter Malone nodded his head to Father King and said, "This is indeed a good start, but there's a long way to go…" He stepped back away from the heat and continued, "Openness and accountability must not be taken for granted. There must be a new system of continual vigilance for the possibility of any type of corruption."

Damian butted in, "In other words…keep an eye out for perverts and pricks…" Peter shook his head in embarrassment for his brother, but the two were unfazed by Damian's rough exterior. Under the sad circumstances of the Archdiocese's previous despicable leadership, Father King showed solidarity when he said, "I fully agree Damian, and I believe the new Bishop is completely with us. He told me we must never let our guard down from the devil within ourselves."

Father Stephen smiled and said, "I like your new Bishop…"

From the edge of the fire barrel, Damian had seen the embers of evil grow until the flames engulfed his childhood friends under the cloak of the fallen clergy. He also knew there may be some sparks of goodness still remaining within the religious system, but if fanned by from a flock who placed their faith in idolization, those sparks could burn out of control. Damian struck the rusty barrel with a boot that rekindled the smoldering flame. With their attention, he said, "I suggest you don't bow down and lick the boots of any man who wears a white collar or high hat, cause remember, we all shit from the same hole."

The crude comment was heard and heeded with a short pause of solidarity from the bowed heads that stared at the receding embers. With the message freshly seared into their souls, Father King continued, "Bishop Murphy has also instructed me, to ask that you stay on as the parish priest. He believes your demonstration of courage and leadership will help in healing process."

"I only did what my conscience dictated."

"Well, the Archdiocese is fortunate to have you as one of our own…"

Without formal notice, Father Malone quickly blurted out, "Father King, I have decided to leave the priesthood and follow my own path."

The Archdiocese priest shook his head and said, "Your absence will be a great loss for us…"

"You already have a priest in your ranks much better than I could ever be. This priest had tried for years to open the eyes of Bishop Stone, but only received punishment from him in the form of banishment." Father King quickly added, "I'm only a new administrator at the Archdiocese…Who is this priest you speak of?"

"Father Andrew Truman has more courage than anyone I know. He stood up to Bishop Stone and was unrightfully removed from this parish."

Father King looked at Peter, and said sincerely, "I will speak to Bishop Murphy today and I promise, it will be rectified."

"One more request, Father King."

"What is it, Father…I mean Peter?"

With his finger pointing in the direction of Father Stephen and wide smile upon his face, Peter asked, "Can you find my friend, a new parish?"

Father Stephen smiled back at his good friend, and said, "That won't be necessary. I have plans to go the missions and spread the good word."

Father King waited for a second and then he asked, "Is there anything else I can do for you, Peter?"

The evening sun was beginning to go down over the graveyard hill. From the priest's house, the sun could be seen turning the white gravestones into red beacons. Peter's face began to reflect the flame from the burning fire, as they looked upon the hill where Justin Morey lay. As the fire softly crackled, Peter said, "Yes, Father King…you can go in peace."

Father Stephen Easton blessed himself and said, "Seems like you are no longer searching my friend. You appear to have found peace in your soul."

Peter looked down upon the burnt vestments and replied, "It's been a long time coming, but I'm almost there…"

His good friend removed a precious wooden cross that hung around his neck and placed it in Peter's hand, and said, "Maybe this will get you the rest of the way…" Peter took the small wooden cross and stared at the burning fire.

Damian looked confidently at his brother, and asked, "What are you waiting for?" Peter took the cross and slowly placed it over the burning fire. Carefully, he singed the bottom of the cross and said, "It will always remind me of our forged friendship and Justin Morey's courageous last stand."

Peter placed his hand on Pat Morey's shoulder, and asked, "Could you give me a ride to the airport?"

"I'll get the bags for you, Father Malone."

"You can call me Peter now."

Pat Morey wiped his tired face and respectfully said, "You'll always be Father Malone to me."

Peter went to shake his friend's hand, but Stephen hugged him instead and asked, "Where will you go?"

Peter glanced at the ashes of Mary Malone's dream that lay in the bottom of the rusty barrel and then looked up at his brother's approving smile. From the pocket of his bright green sweater, Peter presented a ticket to Ireland, and replied, "I'm going to follow my own true path…"